TRICK

TRICK

Treasure Hernandez

www.urbanbooks.net

Urban Books, LLC
300 Farmingdale Road, N.Y.-Route 109
Farmingdale, NY 11735

TRICK Copyright © 2025 Treasure Hernandez

All rights reserved. No part of this book may be reproduced in any form or by any means without prior consent of the Publisher, except brief quotes used in reviews.

To the extent that the image or images on the cover of this book depict a person or persons, such person or persons are merely models, and are not intended to portray any character or characters featured in the book.

ISBN 13: 978-1-64556-712-7
EBOOK ISBN: 978-1-64556-713-4

First Trade Paperback Printing July 2025
Printed in the United States of America

10 9 8 7 6 5 4 3 2 1

This is a work of fiction. Any references or similarities to actual events, real people, living or dead, or to real locales are intended to give the novel a sense of reality. Any similarity in other names, characters, places, and incidents is entirely coincidental.

Distributed by Kensington Publishing Corp.
Submit Orders to:
Customer Service
400 Hahn Road
Westminster, MD 21157-4627
Phone: 1-800-733-3000
Fax: 1-800-659-2436

The authorized representative in the EU for product safety and compliance
Is eucomply OU, Parnu mnt 139b-14, Apt 123
Tallinn, Berlin 11317, hello@eucompliancepartner.com

TRICK

by

Treasure Hernandez

Act One

Prologue

Money, power, or love were usually why people got out of bed in the morning. But me? Revenge was what woke me up. I yearned for the taste of it on my tongue for months, doing whatever I had to do just to get one taste. But you know what they say: plans don't always go as planned. Kind of like how my dad wanted his baby girl to make him proud with some degree in something big. But school was never my thing. I was an art girl.

"Art won't pay the bills. Art will starve you. You're a Halloway, Amber. Never forget that."

My father's voice used to play repeatedly in my head, but it was never loud enough for me to change my course. Sometimes, I thought that if maybe I had listened, things would be different. Maybe I could have been some famous doctor or surgeon and made my entire family proud. But that just wasn't in the cards for me. Sooo, I was what many young women aspired to be . . . a bad bitch. And I'd be lying if I said I didn't love the kind of attention I got when I stepped into a room. I always planned to use my looks to get what I wanted, and that was why I knew my art career would thrive. I had beauty *and* talent. Paired together, I didn't see how I could lose . . . until I lost.

The things about myself that I loved deeply at one point in time were the things I had started to regret as I stared into the barrel of a shiny pistol. Being shapely and sexy as hell with a doll face didn't seem to matter as my life flashed before my eyes. I trembled as my eyes slowly left the gun and traveled up the arm of the person holding it.

"Please, don't," I begged.

"You're his heart, and I want it broken."

His voice was cold and steady. I knew that meant he was standing firm in his decision, and there was nothing I could do. I sat there staring into the familiar face of a man who I loved deeply as he stared back at me with hatred.

"But . . . I love you."

"You don't love shit."

I jumped when I heard the gun cock back and felt warm tears streaming down my face. He didn't care about what I had to say. I was hoping that it wouldn't have to come to that. I was hoping that my gift of gab would save me. I wished I could just go back and change it all. But it was too late. Fate had already played its hand for me, and it was time to sweep the cards off the table. As I stared into his eyes, our time together as kids flashed before mine. It was time to say goodbye, but not before I played the recent weeks back. I took a deep breath and returned to the beginning of it all in my mind.

Chapter One

Amber

"Daddy!" I bustled around our large five-bedroom family home in search of my cell phone.

I'd just had it at breakfast, but when I went to the restroom and came out, it wasn't where I'd placed it. Or where I thought I'd placed it. Sometimes, I did things so automatically I didn't store them in my memory. Like when I came home after a night out, set my purse or keys down somewhere, and didn't remember the next day. I had all but torn the kitchen apart trying to find my phone, and I was starting to think maybe I was crazy. I needed the help of the only other person who was home at the time.

"Daddy!"

"What's wrong, baby?" His voice finally sounded as he came into the kitchen.

He stopped in his tracks when he saw my handiwork in the kitchen. It was then that I took it in too. I'd pulled out every chair from the table, the placemats were on the floor, the jars on the kitchen counter were in disarray, and the island in the center looked like I'd taken my arm and swatted everything off it.

"What the hell . . ."

"I can't find my phone, and I'm going to be late meeting this art dealer if I don't leave now."

"Phone? You mean *this* phone?" He brandished my pink cell phone from his pocket and handed it to me.

"Yes. Where did you find it?" I asked, checking my notifications.

"In the bathroom on the towel rack."

"I must've been moving too fast," I said sheepishly.

"Lina is going to be pissed at you. She worked hard on organizing the island." He shook his head, looking around at the damage I'd caused.

Lina was our housekeeper. She stayed with us but returned to Mexico to visit her family for a week. She was due back today, and I couldn't wait. She wasn't Black, but she sure cooked like it. I'd been almost dying having to fix my own food, and I couldn't even play like my cooking skills came close to hers.

"Can't you just give her a nice bonus or something?" I asked, and Daddy gave me an incredulous look.

"*Excuse* me?"

"Daddy, please. I'm sorry. I'd clean it up if I had the time."

"Oh yeah, I forgot. You're meeting some art dealer in hopes of . . . what exactly?"

"In hopes of showcasing some of my work in his show."

"And who is this dealer?"

"Antonio Rondell. Retired, a renowned artist, and his shows generate millions of dollars. He just had a show in Paris, and one piece alone sold for $700,000."

"Well, if he's so renowned, why is he retired?"

"MS. He physically isn't able to hold a paintbrush anymore so he continues his work by shedding light on other artists. And hopefully, after today, I'll be one of them."

I could tell by the exasperated breath he took and the way he clenched his lips together as if to stop his original thought from escaping he was going to say something to get on my nerves. A part of me hated that his parenting got on my nerves, but the other part wanted him to let me live my life. I understood why he had reservations about me chasing my art dreams. Years ago, my mother left him to raise my brother and me so she could fulfill her dream of being a Broadway singer. I had to have been about 8 at the time of their divorce, and I didn't remember much but my father's sadness. That was when he hired Lina to care for us since he was a high-profile lawyer and needed the help.

I always thought he hoped my mom would come back, but that hope was shattered when she was mugged after one of her greatest shows. She'd just performed in *Hamilton*, and afterward, when she left to meet up with a few of her friends, she was attacked for her purse. My mom was a fighter and wouldn't let go of the bag. The mugger shot her and left her for dead. Well, that was what I was told anyway. I felt like the thought of her lying there like that plagued Daddy's mind so much that he started to blame her career for what the mugger had done. He hated the arts, any form of it.

"When are you going back to school, Amber?" he finally asked. "You're only a few credits away from your degree, and I don't see the point in waiting."

"Daddy, what's the point in getting a degree I won't use?" I said and sighed.

I didn't want to have the "college" talk again. My dad really wanted me to be like him and my older brother, Allun. He'd gotten his nickname "Dawg" at an early age because he was the type to sniff out anything he wanted and any information he needed to know. He'd followed in our father's footsteps and became a lawyer just like him. He even worked for Daddy's firm, where I was expected to work one day. But I didn't want to be a lawyer or anything along those lines. I had my own path, and I wanted to follow that and *only* that. I didn't want to be Supergirl in the day and Batgirl at night.

"You're just like your mother, you know that?"

"I don't think that's a bad thing," I said, kissing his cheek. "Bye, Daddy. I'll see you later, okay?"

He grumbled something under his breath, and I couldn't help but laugh a little as I approached the door. Before I left, I grabbed the painting I hoped Antonio would showcase in his show. It was wrapped and leaning against the wall underneath my hanging purse, which I also grabbed. I bustled out of the house and rushed to where my pink Range Rover was parked in our circular driveway. Pulling out, I checked the dash and saw it was about nine o'clock. Antonio agreed to meet me at a coffee shop downtown at 9:30. I was pushing it, but I was sure I'd get there on time. I would prove my dad and anyone else who doubted me wrong.

Chapter Two

Darryl

I didn't know what to do with that child of mine. Amber had so much potential, but she wasted it chasing a pipe dream. Now, don't get me wrong. The girl was gifted with any kind of drawing or painting tool. However, I wanted her to chase longevity. I didn't want her to waste her most important years on something that wouldn't help build her legacy. Now, the Halloway firm was something she could pass down to her children and her children's children. I'd built my business from the mud up, which was something to be proud of.

Growing up, I lived with my parents. Our home wasn't just dysfunctional; it was chaotic. My father was an abusive alcoholic, and my mother turned to drugs to deal with his abuse. Not only that, but we were also dirt poor. I hated being home on the weekends and in the summer because school was the only place I got consistent hot meals. And that was bad because school wasn't my favorite place either. Although there have been many noticeable changes in the education system since then, I could say that, without a doubt, back then, the education system wasn't meant for Black students to excel. Not to mention the unsupportive teachers. I was nothing but a scruffy kid they tolerated for a paycheck. Between that and my finally being taken away from my parents at age

12, I knew that the only person who could save me from a life of turmoil was me.

The Halloway firm was a testament to my struggles and my success. I didn't understand why Amber wanted no part of it. What she didn't know was that she didn't have a choice, and I was putting my foot down. The only reason she felt free enough to gallivant around doing what she wanted to do was because she was on my dime. I paid for every part of the lifestyle she loved so much. It was June, and I expected her to reregister for school by July first and finish her degree, or else she could kiss her lifestyle goodbye. I would never put my child on the streets. I would put her in a simple apartment and downgrade her car to something she could afford, working whatever low-paying job she could find. Some might call me harsh, but I would disagree. I refused to work hard while my child just lived off the fat of the land.

I pushed my disappointed thoughts about my daughter out of my head and sat at the table to sip my morning coffee. While doing so, I checked the messages on my phone. My son, Dawg, reminded me that we had to meet a client this morning. He was always on his toes, but I was always a few steps ahead of him. I would never forget about a meeting with a high-profile client like Theodore Lavy, the oldest of the Lavy brothers. He was currently fighting a gun charge and attempted murder. It wouldn't have been a tough case if it weren't for the fact that he was already a convicted felon and wasn't supposed to have a gun in the first place.

While the prosecution was building a case against him, Dawg and I were putting together our defense, which demanded we work tirelessly. See, the Lavy brothers owned a lot of property in Atlanta, and it was said that they were also underground drug traffickers as well. That side hadn't surfaced yet, so I wasn't sure how true it was.

However, if I were to find out it *was* true, I'd drop him as a client. I'd experienced firsthand how drugs can ruin a person's life, and I wouldn't defend the freedom of a man poisoning the world. I finished my coffee and prepared to get up from the table when I heard the front door open and close.

"Mr. Halloway, I'm back. I—" Lina stopped midsentence when she entered the kitchen and looked around. "Oh my God. Was the place robbed?"

I couldn't help but to laugh at her wide eyes as she looked around at Amber's handiwork. Lina was a petite woman who looked more like a fresh 31-year-old than a woman pushing 50 years. Her dark brunette hair usually stayed in a single French braid, and she, like Amber, stayed on top of her beauty regimens. Her nails and eyelashes were always freshly done, and she wore just enough makeup to give her a glow. Nothing more, nothing less.

"No, no. The place wasn't robbed, Lina. It was that daughter of mine looking for her phone."

"That damn girl," Lina groaned. "I thought I'd have time to unpack and rest a little."

"How about a nice tip for this mess, and you take the rest of the day off? You can start your full regular shift tomorrow," I said and handed her $200 from my wallet.

"Thank you, Mr. Halloway, but I'm afraid I won't be able to take the full day off. The kids clearly couldn't wait for me to return from Mexico." She chuckled and shook her head. "Dawg called me as soon as my flight landed and wants me to come clean his condo today."

"You *do* know you were gone for a week, right?" I said, thinking about what creatures she might encounter when she walked into my son's place.

"I know. And I have my gloves ready," she said jokingly.

"Thanks, Lina." I got up from the table and gave her a quick kiss on the forehead before grabbing my briefcase.

"Have a good day," she called after me.

I left the house with a smile on my face. I hadn't realized just how much I'd missed her until she was back at home. Lina had come into my life when I needed her the most. As a newly widowed man with two children and a career, I needed a miracle. And that miracle came in the form of a feisty, sharp-tongued woman. She helped me raise my children while keeping me sane at the same time. Although some people mistook us for a married couple over the years, Lina and I were more like brother and sister. I didn't know what I would have done without her.

I drove my freshly washed Benz CLE AMG coupe to the office, listening to some Run-DMC and LL. Real music. I didn't know any of the trash the kids listened to these days. I just knew it wasn't for me. When I got to the firm, I did what I always did when I arrived. I parked in my designated spot right by the door and looked up at the beautiful two-story building. Dawg and I weren't the only lawyers the firm had. We had three more of the brightest minds Atlanta had to offer. Tiana Campbell specialized in family law and was a shark at what she did. Gaven Holt specialized in corporate law, while Anthony Sinclaire covered all our civil cases. Dawg and I handled every defense case, and he was also a senior partner of the company.

After taking in my masterpiece for what felt like the millionth time, I got out of my car and went inside. We all had our own personal secretaries, and mine was waiting for me at his desk right outside of my office. Jeffrey was a flamboyantly gay man dressed like he was showing up to a fashion show every day at work. He had a light complexion and wore designer prescription glasses on his overly chiseled face. The truth was, I didn't give a damn about his lifestyle or who he was sleeping with. All I cared about was him doing an effective job for me . . . which he did flawlessly. He had graduated top of his class and had an accounting degree, meaning he was paid more than the average secretary.

"Good morning, Mr. Halloway," he greeted me, looking up from his computer screen.

"Good morning, Jeff. Anything for me?"

"Yes. I put some paperwork you need to go over and sign before I can fax it back. Also, the Jacksons have sent the firm their final payment of $100,000. Would you like me to transfer that into your primary personal account or leave it be?"

"Leave it be for now. That will probably end up going to Amber's tuition."

I stepped into my office, but not before catching the raised brow Jeffrey gave me. I hadn't even gotten comfortable in my chair before he came in, tapping his pen on his notepad. Knowing he only did that when something was taxing his mind, I sighed.

"What is it, Jeffrey?"

"I couldn't help but *think* I heard you say something about Amber's tuition?"

"Yeah, what about it?"

"I thought she dropped out to pursue her art career."

"She took a break. She didn't drop out."

"Mm . . . Well, does *she* know that?"

I cut my eyes at him. He'd been working for me for over a decade and had become something like a nephew to me. I want to say that his forwardness had just started, but Jeffrey had always been the all-or-nothing type. He was respectful for the most part, but he didn't hold his tongue, even when he should have.

"And what is that supposed to mean?"

"I'm just saying Amber is different. She's the *Gone with the Wind* type, not the clock-in-at-eight-o'clock-sharp type. Maybe it's time you just accept her for who she is."

"What the hell would you know about it? You don't have any kids."

"But I *am* somebody's kid. My parents disagree with my lifestyle to this day, and it hurts because I love them. When they cut me off and left me out in the world all alone, it cut me deeply. A part of me feels like now, they don't accept me because I never 'learned my lesson.'" He made air quotes. "Instead, I showed them I can survive without them. But I know you wouldn't do anything like that, right? You'd never cut off Amber."

His words made me feel slightly guilty about the things I'd been thinking about doing when it came to Amber. I thought some tough love might get her back on track. But now I was wondering whose track that would be exactly.

"No . . . never," I finally said, and he pursed his lips at me.

"Mmm, good. Because the Highland apartments called back about your inquiry, and I told them never to call here again."

"What? Why would you do that?"

"Because you were tryin'a put my girl up in that raggedy motherfucka. Oh, and I know about the Honda too. A *Honda?* Really, Mr. Halloway? I'm not tryin'a be all up in your business, but uh-uh. You tryin'a kill that girl."

The deep belly laugh came out of my mouth before I could stop it. Mainly because the apartment wasn't terrible, but I knew Amber would hate it and that it wasn't updated. As far as the Honda, it was a step back from what she was used to, but it *was* a very nice car.

"There is nothing wrong with a Honda, Jeff. She would learn to appreciate the luxuries that are so normal to her and work harder to get them back."

"But who's to say she isn't working hard? I think you should hold off on this evilness you tryin'a do and give her another year pursuing her art. And actually *support* her. You'll be surprised what she can do with an anchor in her life."

"We'll see."

"All right." Jeffrey shook his head and looked down at his notepad. "It looks like you have a ten o'clock today. I'll ensure the meeting room is available for you and Allun."

"Speaking of Dawg, is he here?"

"Not yet, but I'm sure he will be soon."

"Hmm . . . This is the fifth time he's been late to work in a month."

"And not to be messy, but he for sure ain't staying later to make up the time. That boy be out of here as soon as the clock hits five."

"I need you to find out what's going on."

"Okay, I'll go on yet another mission for you."

"Well then, let's add one more onto that. I need you to go to the hospital and check on Michael Tony. Something about what Theo is telling me isn't adding up, and without the complete truth, I can't build a solid case of defense. And you know I always make it worth your while."

"You do, and as far as Dawg is concerned, this could be something as simple as seeing someone and wanting to spend a little extra time laid up in the morning. But if you want me to take your money, I will." Jeffrey shrugged and left the office.

   Seeing someone or not, Dawg knew the company came first. His showing up late all of a sudden could send the wrong message to the others in the firm. I didn't want anyone to think I condoned him doing whatever he wanted. And I didn't want them to follow his example. Efficiency was just one of the reasons we were one of the top firms in Atlanta, and that was something that wouldn't change any time soon. I reached for my desk phone and called him to tell him to get his black ass in the office ASAP.

Chapter Three

Dawg

I firmly believed that what someone didn't know couldn't hurt them. And that was what I constantly told myself about the secrets I kept from my family . . . especially my dad. If he knew what I was doing, he would never have agreed with it. In fact, he would be the reason everything came tumbling down, but it was a risk I was willing to take. See, everyone thought that growing up as the son of a hotshot lawyer was everything and more. Although I did have nice things and went to the best schools, I wanted more. And after that, I wanted even more. The top wasn't high enough for me.

Following in Pop's footsteps was something that was just expected of me. Become a lawyer, win high-profile cases, and one day, take over the company. All of that was fine and dandy, but not once had anybody asked me what *I* wanted to be in life. Hell, if they did, I probably wouldn't have even been able to answer back then because I was so busy being groomed to be just like him that I never took the time to think about it. But eventually, it came to me.

In school, although my father thought I was an upstanding student, I did things on the side that he wouldn't be too proud of. Even though I went to private schools, some kids there dealt on the side. Weed, pills, cocaine, all that good stuff. They made their own money and were their own men . . . well, young men. My best friend back then was Jimmy Falco, who was what most would call "the plug" at school. His older brother was Jake Falco, and he weighed heavy in the streets. He was a big-time hustler and provided Jimmy with anything he needed. One day, I asked Jimmy why he sold drugs when he didn't have to. He was a straight-A student and sure to get a scholarship to any school he wanted to attend.

"My mama don't want me to be nothing like Jake. That's why she pulls all those doubles at the hospital to keep me in the expensive-ass school. She don't know that I'm already just like Jake, a hustler," he told me. "One day she not gon' have to work at all, and no school or degree is gon' help me do that. And even if it did, that shit gon' take too long. So, in the meantime, I'ma play the game these crackers want me to play. Because one day, I'ma be the biggest hustler in the game. A wolf hiding in corporate America. Untouchable like a ghost."

To reiterate, being a drug dealer truly just came to me. I never planned on being one, but once I started helping Jimmy flip his packs and seeing how fast the money came in, I got addicted. By the time I was 18 and in my first year of college, I'd already saved up a hundred thousand dollars of my own money. My father, who was always busy at work, never questioned me when I was often gone. He figured I was just a normal college kid doing normal college kid things. His radar didn't go off as long as I was making good grades and passing all my classes. However, soon, my production picked up, and it was too much to hide in my room at our family home. Not only that, but Lina also started snooping around my room more. I knew it was time to leave. I decided to move out and get my own place, which wasn't suspicious since I was a man then.

When Jake was killed in a deal gone wrong, Jimmy and I took over as head of his operation. Jimmy had long left his dream of being a corporate kingpin in high school. He never went to college and, instead, dived deeper into the streets. Jimmy was a great hustler, but he wasn't that good of a businessman. That's where I came in. Although Jimmy was the face of the operation in Atlanta, I was the brains. Nothing ran without me. As I said, Jimmy wasn't much of an executive. He could move a pack quicker than someone could blink their eyes, but he had an anger problem. He knew nothing of order. He only wanted power, and that way of thinking had almost cost us our Cuban plug, Benny.

Benny was Jake's connect who lived in Florida. Once a month, Jake took a trip and hauled back the product. Without Benny, we had no operation, especially at the price point he gave us. However, he refused to do business with Jimmy despite his being Jake's brother. So I had to make the monthly trip instead, which was why I was late getting to the office again.

I'd just returned to town the night before and dropped the product off at our warehouse. Before I went to bed, I made sure to text my dad about work so he felt I was still locked in our case. As fate would have it, I slept through my alarm and woke to my cell phone ringing.

"Hello?" I answered after snatching it off the nightstand.

"Where the hell are you?" My father's stern voice came through the phone.

"I'm walking out the door now," I lied, jumping out of bed.

"You should already be here. You were the one who reminded me about the meeting we have today. Theo Lavy is paying us a lot of money to have us represent him."

"I know, Pop."

"Do you? Or maybe you just don't care. I haven't forgotten how adamant you were about us *not* representing him."

"Pop, I'm coming."

"You better be."

He hung up before I could tell him goodbye. I stared at the phone for a second before throwing my head up at the ceiling and groaning loudly. Living a double life was starting to catch up with me. I kept telling myself that after a few more years, I would step away from the firm and invest in businesses that made me money without having to do too much. I was hoping that my baby sister would finally go and finish law school so that she could take my place, but that was just wishful thinking. The last thing she wanted to do was be like me or our father, and I couldn't blame her.

I quickly showered, then threw on a suit and tie before grabbing my briefcase and jetting out of the house. I hit the gas on my Dodge Charger and fought against traffic to make it to the firm in time. Theo Lavy was a very precise man. He was the oldest of three boys, and my father was right about me not wanting to represent him. My father only knew what Theo *wanted* him to know . . . that he was a reformed businessman with a hard past. His case was pretty straightforward. His home was broken into, and he shot the man. Where it got sticky was the fact that Theo wasn't supposed to have any weapons. And after detectives dug more into the shooting, they couldn't find any sign of forced entry or a motive for the break-in. The man Theo shot was still in a coma and was being watched around the clock so the detectives could question him when he woke up. They didn't believe it was a break-in, and if they could prove it wasn't, Theo was as good as locked up.

The judge he had was a tough one, especially to ex-offenders who happened to be Black males. The gun Theo had used to shoot the man was registered in his girlfriend's name. They were trying to prove that Theo not only had constructive possession of the gun but that his girlfriend had also explicitly purchased it for him. What should have been an easy case was proving to be a doozy, especially with the attempted murder.

"Hey, Jeff, where's Pop?" I asked after finally arriving at the firm.

I first went to Pop's office to find him, but he wasn't there. Jeff was sitting at his desk typing something into the computer. He looked up at me and pursed his lips while shaking his head.

"Where you think he's at? In the meeting room where you should be. Go!"

I left him there and went through the fancy building to the main meeting room we used for clients. When I stepped inside, I saw Pop sitting across from Theo. As always, Pop was crisp in a nice suit. The graying beard on his face matched the gray hair on his neatly trimmed head. His gold cuff links went well with the Rolex timepiece on his wrist. I'd like to think I got my sense of style from him, but Amber helped us both keep up with the times. Theo sat across from him, dressed casually in street clothes. Like me, he was a brown-skinned man in his early thirties and had a headful of curly hair. He turned around when he heard the door open and close to see who it was.

"You're late," my father said in an annoyed tone that annoyed me.

"My apologies. Traffic," I said evenly, keeping my composure. I sat down beside my father, avoiding his eyes, and picked up some of the paperwork on the table separating us from Theo. "Where were we?"

"I was just telling Theo that not much has changed with the status of his case," Pop started. "Except them now saying that they don't see any of his girlfriend Teesha Pedal's fingerprints on the weapon."

"And what's that supposed to mean?" Theo asked.

"It means they're going to double down on the fact that she bought the gun for you and that it was never intended for personal use for her," I explained, and Theo smacked his lips.

"Man, they can't prove that shit. She could have cleaned it."

"But that doesn't explain why only *your* fingerprints are on the bullets," Pop told him, and Theo leaned back in his seat.

"So, what now? I know I ain't pay no $20,000 retainer fee to be told I'm going to jail."

"I pose that we say that upon hearing the intruder in your home, you did what you had to do to protect your family. You grabbed the gun from its compartment and loaded it before you went downstairs to see who was in your home."

"They ain't gon' believe that shit."

"It's a long shot, but it's what we have to go based on what we have."

"Until that snake-ass motherfucka Michael Tony wakes his ass up. *If* he does anyway."

"Well, if it's true that he was breaking into the house, we shouldn't have anything to worry about, right?" Pop asked, but Theo didn't answer. "Theo, is there something you aren't telling us? Because we can't represent you to the fullest if you're keeping secrets."

"Yeah, he tried to rob me. That's the truth."

Something about the way he answered the question made me feel that there was, in fact, something he was hiding. However, if he wasn't forthcoming, there wasn't anything we could do for the moment. He and my father continued talking, and I leaned back, trying to listen, but I felt myself zoning out. I thought of Jimmy and how he would feel if he knew that the firm was representing one of the Lavy brothers, our enemy and competition. Granted, Theo knew nothing of who I really was, but I knew a lot about him and his family. Like how all the businesses, including their popular club Razberry, were all just a front for who they really were. The whispers about them were true. They were self-proclaimed drug kingpins and extremely dangerous. Word had it that Theo was the one who pulled the trigger on Jake due to an ongoing war for territory. Atlanta was big but not big enough to have two kingpins on the same level. It made sense that he wanted to get rid of the competition. He just hadn't bet on Jimmy quickly taking Jake's place. We were at war with them, which was why I had all but begged Pop not to take on the case. It was too messy. However, since I couldn't talk him out of it, I was trying to figure out how to use this closeness to him to my advantage.

"We'll be in touch," I heard Pop say, and I snapped back to reality.

He and Theo stood up and shook hands in farewell. I followed suit and extended my own hand to Theo. Instead of taking it, he looked at it and then back at me.

"Be on time, next time. I'm not paying all this money for any flunkies."

His words were harsh, but I couldn't say they shocked me. I lowered my hand and forced a smile on my lips. I nodded.

"Of course, Mr. Lavy," was all I said.

After eyeing me for a second more, Theo turned and left the meeting room. When he was gone, Pop turned to me and looked disappointed. It was the same look he gave me when I was a kid, and he felt I hadn't done a good enough job on something. Not wanting to be lectured, I made to leave the room too, but he stopped me.

"What's going on with you, son?" he asked, and I held in my groan.

"Nothing, Pop. I'm fine."

"You sure about that? You've been late multiple times this month, and today was most embarrassing. It's one thing to be late, but it's another to have this firm look incompetent."

"How do we look incompetent? I showed up, and truly, I'm just helping you out on this one. It's your case. I didn't even want to take him on as a client. I told you that."

"You *told* me that, huh?" Pop scoffed at my bold statement. "Well, how about you tell me what the hell is going on in your life that's throwing you off the focus of your legacy? Is it a woman?"

"If I was seeing someone, you would know, Pop. Nothing is going on with me."

"Then get your damn head in the game. And I mean it. All this will be yours one day. Don't forget that."

He gave me another stern look before he left the room. I stuffed my hands into my pocket and took a deep breath. Sometimes, I didn't think he understood the weight he was trying to hand off to me.

Chapter Four

Amber

I sent a prayer of thanks up to God when I made it on time to Mocha Dips, the coffee shop Antonio agreed to meet me at. It was a popular place, and almost every table was occupied when I walked inside the establishment. Holding my painting, I scanned the crowd for Antonio before spotting him in the back corner at a table by himself. He was a stylish Black man in his midforties and wore rectangular glasses. His legs were crossed underneath the table as he peacefully sipped his coffee. I couldn't tell just by looking at him if he was straight or not. The artsy types were always hard to read. My feet moved before my mind told them to. I must have been moving a little too quickly because the next thing I knew, the left side of my body bumped into someone, and I felt cold liquid splash on my arm.

"My bad. I ain't even see you," a deep voice said.

I was so thrown off by the coffee sliding down my arm I hadn't even looked to see who I'd run into. When I did, I had to look up because the man towered over me. He had smooth, peanut butter-colored skin and wore his curly hair down over his face. His full lips and pointed nose gave him a distinctive look, but his hazel eyes were his moneymakers, for sure. He was holding a drink in his hand. Our collision had caused the top to pop off, and I wasn't the only one the drink had done damage to. His white shirt was stained, although he dabbed at it with some napkins in his hand.

"No, it's me who should be sorry. I wasn't watching where I was going," I said.

"Here," he said, handing me some napkins, so I wiped off my arm. He noticed the painting in my hand. "I ain't fuck that up, did I?"

"No, I think it's good," I said after looking down at the canvas painting hanging in my right hand. I was relieved that it was okay.

"Good. Can I buy you a coffee or something?"

"Um," I looked at Antonio and saw him check his watch. I looked back at the hazel-eyed man and gave him a regretful smile. "I'm actually meeting someone here. Thank you, though."

Before he could say anything else, I walked away. The last thing I needed was my opportunity with Antonio to slip between my fingers. On my way to the table, I tossed the crumpled-up napkins in my hand in a trash can I passed. I confidently walked up to Antonio, and when he noticed me, he smiled.

"I was starting to wonder if you would be a no-show."

"I'm so sorry. I thought I could beat Atlanta traffic, but that was wishful thinking."

"No problem. Please sit." He motioned to the chair across from him.

When I did, I noticed the hazel-eyed man still standing there staring at me. There was something about the way his eyes lingered on me that made my stomach do cartwheels. I cleared my throat and broke eye contact, focusing all my attention on Antonio.

"Thank you for meeting with me today. Your showcases are amazing."

"They are. Thank you. When I first started, it was a showcase that put me on the map. So, it gives me great pleasure to be able to offer exposure to artists all over the world."

At that moment, a waitress came over to take my order, but I turned her away. I was so anxious I didn't want to put anything else on top of the breakfast in my stomach. Before I turned back to Antonio, I glanced quickly at where the hazel-eyed man had been standing and saw that he was gone. He probably had to change his shirt.

"I understand you want one of your pieces to be included in this weekend's showcase?" Antonio asked.

"Yes," I said and felt my eyes light up at the thought.

"Well, tell me a little about yourself before you show me your painting. That way, when I see it, I can feel it."

"Okay. Um, where do I start?"

"Tell me about your parents. Who are they? What do they do?"

"Well, my father is a lawyer, and he's been one my whole life."

"Mm, so away at work all the time?" Antonio asked.

"I guess you can say that. He has his own firm, so much of his attention must go there. He wants my brother and me to take it over one day, but that's just not the life I see for myself."

"Aah. Father wants children to take over his dynasty, but children want to create their own. Interesting."

"My brother wants to take it over, and he can. But I don't see myself as a lawyer. I'm an artist. While Daddy was at work and my brother was doing whatever, I was always in the house with our nanny, painting or drawing something. I loved bringing my thoughts to life."

"Hmm . . . Nanny? Where was your mother?"

"She . . . She died. Years ago when I was little. Umm, she was a Broadway singer and left to follow her dreams. She had the most beautiful voice."

"How did she die?" Antonio asked, digging deeper.

The question threw me off. Most people didn't ask how if I didn't offer the information. I was staring at Antonio, but my mind went to the last time I saw my mother. She'd just finished packing her bags to be on the road again for a few weeks, and I remembered how I clung to her.

"Please don't go, Mommy. Stay here and sing to me. You don't have to go."

She stood there in her long, elegant coat with matching gloves and hat, wearing an annoyed look. She was rushing to leave so she wouldn't miss her flight. She cupped my face with her hands and gave me a quick kiss on the forehead.

"Mommy will be back sooner than you know it. Okay?"

"But why do you have to go? Don't you like us?"

"Baby, I love you, but I love my dream too. And I have to follow it. One day, you'll understand." She pried me off her legs and kissed Dawg before embracing my father. Within moments, she was out the door.

I snapped back to reality and took a steady breath to keep the tears threatening to fall at bay. The next time I saw my mother after that was in her coffin. It was hard to think or talk about her, especially since it was something that neither my father nor Dawg ever brought up. But there I was, talking about her to a stranger.

"Um . . . She was mugged in New York after a show."

"What was her name?"

"Fanny . . . Fanny Halloway."

At the mention of her name, Antonio's eyes grew wide.

"Fanny Halloway was your *mother?*" he breathed, and I nodded. "Oh, honey, I had the pleasure of hearing her sing years before she was on Broadway."

"Really?"

"Yes, my dear. It was, I believe, 1998, inside a shop similar to this one. She blew me away. I knew she would be a star, so when she became one, I wasn't surprised. Such a shame a talent like that was taken so terribly. And another thing—" He surprised me by reaching across the table and squeezing my hand. "Tears are art because art is nothing but emotion we can externally see. If they need to flow, let them flow."

I heard him loud and clear, but I still wouldn't allow my tears to hit my cheeks. All I could offer was a smile and a nod. He watched me intensely, and I almost wanted to avert my eyes, but something told me not to.

"I could cry every day if I wanted to, but that won't bring her back," I said. "To me, my art is a way to pay homage to my lineage, and there are certain people I wish would understand that. But some things you can't force."

"Beautifully put. You're quite intriguing, Amber Halloway. I just can't quite put a finger on why yet. How about we take a look at your painting, shall we?"

I didn't think he would ever ask. I carefully took the cloth from over the canvas painting and slid it over to him. He picked it up with both hands and held it up to get a better vision of it. I looked at it with him as if I were looking at it for the first time. I'd painted a woman on a cliff looking down onto a village. Half of the painting was the day, and the other half was the night. I couldn't tell if he was impressed just by looking at his face.

"What does this mean to you?" Antonio asked.

"To me, it represents new hope. Each day brings new possibilities, no matter how hard getting through the night is. But . . ."

"But what?"

"My representation doesn't really matter. I could tell you why I did this or that all day, but you'll always form your own meaning for something that touches you. I don't want to control the narrative for any potential consumer's take on the art they're drawn to."

The smile that came to Antonio's face was slow, but it ended wide. He stared at the painting for a few more moments before handing it back to me. My heart fluttered, and I crossed my fingers underneath the table.

"Amber, it's been a while since someone has moved me with their words. But your words have been paired with real talent. I would be honored to present your painting at my event."

"Seriously?" I asked breathlessly.

"Ask my husband. I don't joke about things like this, darling," he said.

"Oh my God, this is so amazing. Thank you. Thank you so much. You have no idea how much this means to me."

"I'll send you an email detailing the event. They usually are jampacked, but you will be allowed a plus-one. Also, to ensure that all my artists' proceeds are fair and just, I don't disclose who created what until the bid is made."

"I completely understand. I just . . . I can't believe this."

The excitement raging through my body was almost too much to handle. I tried to keep my composure so I wouldn't look like a lunatic. But really, I wanted to leap for joy all around that coffee shop.

"Well, believe it," he said. "Please bring this painting an hour before the showcase this weekend."

"Okay. Thank you."

"No, thank *you*."

He dipped his head and got up, leaving his drink on the table. Still in a daze, I watched him leave the coffee shop. I looked at my painting again and realized it was just the beginning. I still had to sell it. However, if Antonio thought it was good enough to showcase, I had high hopes. I grinned, placing the cloth cover back over it and standing up to leave.

I was on a natural high when I walked out of the coffee shop and made my way to my car. When I got there, I was shocked to see the hazel-eyed man leaning on it like he owned it. I furrowed my brow and put my free hand on my hip.

"*Excuse* you?" I asked, and he laughed.

"I knew this was yo' whip."

"So, that gives you the right to lean on my shit?"

"Nah, I just wanted to be here when you got done with your little meeting or whatever."

"And why is that?" I asked and rolled my eyes.

"'Cause you ain't let me buy a coffee. I wanted to know what you got on for the rest of the day."

"That's how you ask a girl on a date?"

"Ones who casually ruin a $200 shirt, yeah." He pointed to the dried stain on his shirt.

"That was an accident."

"Well, me being on yo' car ain't."

I wanted to curse him out so badly. I wanted to read him for filth . . . leaning on my freshly washed car like he owned it or something. But I couldn't. I couldn't even fight the smile that made my cheeks lift. I didn't know what, but there was just something about him.

"You don't even know my name."

"And you don't know mine, either," he responded.

"So who's going to ask first?"

"I'm a gentleman, so I will. What's your name, beautiful?"

"I don't know if I should tell you now. Waiting for me like this is kind of much."

"Nah, this pressure, shawty," he said smoothly, making me smile again.

"Mmm . . . Well, my name is Amber," I said, and he flashed his pearly whites.

"Amber? I like that. I'm Myleek. Leek for short."

"Okay. Well, Leek, can you get off my car?"

"If you let me take you out," he said, and I rolled my eyes.

"When?" I asked, trying to force the attitude in my voice.

"Tonight. You don't even have to give me your number yet. Just meet me in this exact spot at eight o'clock."

"Eight o'clock?" I asked, and he nodded.

I contemplated the proposal while looking him up and down. Minus the stain on his shirt, he was clean. He was rocking the newest Jordans, a nice pair of jeans, and had a designer belt bag across his chest that matched his designer belt. I didn't have to ask to know a gun was probably in it. I knew I should have said no, but the scent of his cologne was as enticing as his smile. It was like an invisible mist saying, "Come to me." Plus, bad boys were always my favorite.

"Fine . . . I'll be here. But if I don't see you, I'm pulling off."

"Bet," he said and winked at me before getting off my car and walking away.

I didn't realize I was still smiling until I got inside the car and looked in my rearview mirror. Once I noticed, I stopped immediately. I was used to men flirting with me, but I wasn't used to anyone being so bold. As I pulled away, I tried to play my music, but it cut off as soon as I turned it on because a call was trying to come through. I almost ignored it until I saw it was Dawg.

"Hello?" I answered, excited to tell him about Antonio and the showcase.

"Sis, where you at?"

"In traffic. You?"

"At the office. Pop tripping again. I was late."

"Then duh, he's tripping," I said.

"He gon' be tripping a lot more because I have to leave. I need you, though."

"What's up?"

"I need you to meet me at Lakeside tonight. Can you?"

"Yup. I'll be there."

Chapter Five

Dawg

The Past

I hated having to show my hand, but I often had to because people tried to play me because I was 17. To me, age meant nothing in business. Especially when it was me a person came to for product. And by "person," I meant Brian Oneal. Ever since Jake had put me and Jimmy on, Brian had been coming to us for his product. I told Jimmy I didn't trust him, but Jimmy often overlooked it because he was too focused on the money. And because Brian usually paid up front, he didn't think anything of it when he asked us to front him fifteen pounds of weed.

That evening, it was time to collect the paper because Brian had been late with his payment. It was up to me to do it since Jake and Jimmy were out of town. I wasn't tripping, though. It was something to keep my mind busy since my mama's funeral. I knew Pop wasn't okay, but he hadn't discussed it. I knew I wasn't okay because I couldn't talk about it. Pop had drowned himself in work, and I'd barely seen him in the past weeks. It was up to me to be strong for my baby sister. That night, I planned on leaving her with Lina to make my run and then come back and watch her favorite movie with her.

However, an unfortunate event changed those plans. And by "unfortunate event," I meant Amber herself.

"What the hell are you doing?" I asked when I stepped back into my bedroom fully dressed after taking a hot shower.

I realized my bedroom door was wide open as I walked back to it from the hallway. I could have sworn I shut it, especially since I had a nosy 12-year-old sister running around the house. Sure enough, there she was, standing over my bed wearing her favorite Winnie the Pooh sweatshirt. Her head was down, and she was digging in the book bag I had sitting on the bed waiting for me. My heart dropped when I saw that she was holding my loaded pistol. I hurried to snatch and tuck it into my sweatpants. She didn't even flinch.

"Why do you have a gun?" she asked.

"Because I do. Don't be going through my stuff, Tink," I said, calling her by the nickname Mama had given her when she was a baby since she tinkered with everything.

"Why?"

"Because it's my stuff."

"No, I think you just didn't want me to see the drugs you have in that bag," she said with a shrug.

"I don't know what you're talking about," I said. I tried to act clueless, although I knew to get to the gun in her hand, she had to dig past the drugs in the bag. I grabbed my bag from the bed and tucked the pistol back inside it.

"You don't?" she asked.

"Nope."

"Then what's this?" She walked over to a small shelf on my wall and slid it over like she'd done it before.

I was stunned when she pointed to the hole I'd made in the wall to stash my drugs behind the shelf. I planned to fix it whenever I moved out, and I never thought anyone would ever find it.

"How—"

"I've known for a long time now. You and Daddy always leave me here alone with Lina, so I go through your stuff. You aren't the only one with secrets. Daddy secretly smokes cigarettes."

"It's wrong to go through someone's stuff, Amber."

"My name ain't Tink for nothing." She shrugged.

I let out an annoyed breath and moved the shelf back in place so that the secret hole in the wall was fully covered again. When I looked back at my sister, she had a mischievous look on her face. I didn't know what it meant, but knew it wasn't good.

"You can't tell anyone about my gun or what you've seen. Understand? Pop won't understand."

"I coulda been ratted you out, but I didn't. You're my brother."

"Good," I said, relieved.

"But . . ."

"But what?"

"What if I accidentally say something? I'm not saying I will, but what if I'm just talking to Daddy, and it just . . . slips?"

"What do you want so it won't slip?" I asked the little monster.

"I wanna come with you tonight wherever you're going."

"No deal. Where I'm going isn't a place for kids. How about I double your allowance for a month?"

"No, I want to get out of this house. You and Daddy keep leaving me here with Lina. If you don't take me, you can just consider the beans good as spilled." She shrugged again and started toward the door.

I thought quickly, trying to come up with another compromise, but I knew there was nothing else she would want. I hoped she wouldn't rat me out, especially knowing how much our father hated drugs. However,

I didn't want to take the chance. There was no telling where her state of mind was at the moment, and in a way, I felt bad for her. Pop and I hadn't just been avoiding each other; we'd also neglected Amber in our grief. I played with the thought of letting her come on my run with me. If she stayed in the car, I didn't see how it would hurt any.

"Fine," I said. "But you're staying in the car."

"Cool," she said, whipping back around to face me. "Can we get ice cream on the way?"

"Sure. But you can't say anything to Pop—ever. Do you understand me?"

She nodded, and I threw the book bag on my back. I shook my head as I walked past her out of my room. She rushed to her own bedroom and put on a pair of shoes and a jacket before meeting me outside in the car. I couldn't believe I had gotten hustled by a 12-year-old. Maybe she was more like me than I thought.

Brian had asked me to meet him in the parking lot of the Honey Pot, a sleazy motel known for the ladies of the night who frequented it. Whether he was indulging was beyond me and his own business. All I knew was he had better have my money and all of it. I stopped and got Amber some ice cream like she had asked before I pulled into the parking lot. It was the biggest serving-size bowl they had. I let her load it with whatever she wanted, hoping it would keep her occupied in the car while I went in and handled business.

"Look, stay in this car. Don't get out, no matter what happens. Do you hear me?" I told her, and she rolled her eyes at me.

"What I'ma get out the car for? Ain't those prostitutes?" she asked and pointed at women wearing barely-there garments walking up the steps to their various rooms.

"What you know about a prostitute?" I asked, holding back my laugh.

"I know they do that thang for some change, and those girls look like the type. And I don't want no parts of that."

I couldn't hold my laugh back anymore. I let it out. Amber was the funniest person I knew. She didn't hold her tongue for anything or anybody. Some said she was too grown for her age. I just felt she was expressive. Before Mama died, she wasn't really around to teach her the ways of a young lady, so she became who she wanted to be.

"Look, just stay in the car," I said after parking.

I gave her one last look before grabbing the bag and getting out. As I walked, I checked my phone and saw a text from Brian telling me which room to go to. I glanced back to my car and saw Amber stuffing her face through the window.

"Hey, baby, you wanna have a good time?" one of the women asked me as I made my way up the stairs.

She would have been pretty if it weren't for the small cluster of bumps near her top lip. She'd tried to cover it up with makeup, but I could see them all too well under the lighting of the stairs. I didn't even acknowledge her question. I just continued up the stairs. As I walked, I noticed that every camera on the building was broken. No surveillance made it the perfect place to make any kind of transaction.

Brian's room was on the second floor, and when I got there, I knocked. The door swung open moments later, and Gator, Brian's right-hand man, met me. He nodded at me and stepped back so I could come in. Brian was standing there in the rinky-dink on his phone, smoking a blunt. When he looked up and saw me, he smiled.

"Just the nigga I wanted to see," he said and offered the blunt to me.

"Nah, I got someone waiting for me. I'm just here to get in and out," I told him.

He shrugged and put the blunt out in an ashtray. Then he went to a small closet in the room and pulled out a duffle bag. He tossed it my way, and I unzipped it to count the money inside.

"I need more. Same as last time," he said right when I counted $25,000.

"This is what you owe from last time. If you want more, you gotta up this to fifty. No more fronts," I said.

"Nigga, you know I'm good for it."

"Nah, I know you were late. I don't like late. I like good business."

"You tryin'a say I don't do good business?"

"I'm saying you were late," I said, putting the bag on my back. "You got the other twenty-five? If so, we can make something happen. If not, I'm about to take this money and go."

Brian didn't say anything at first, but his glare was loud enough by itself. Finally, he chuckled slightly, but no jokes were made, and I didn't see anything funny. He looked at Gator, who was standing to my left.

"Nah," Brian finally said. "I don't think you're going anywhere."

Beside me, Gator pulled a gun from his pants and cocked it menacingly. I looked from him and then back to Brian, who now had his arms crossed in bosslike fashion. He nodded his head at the bag in my hand.

"I'ma take them drugs and that twenty-five back. And I'll be nice enough to give your parents an open casket."

"You think Jake won't know it was you?" I asked.

"I don't give a fuck what Jake gon' know. I used him just like I used you and came up doing so. Theo Lavy is making just as much paper, and I'm thinking about getting down with him anyway."

Gator's gun being on me made it risky for me to reach for my own. He would shoot before I could even get a grip on it. My mind went to Amber outside in the car. We'd just lost Mama. She couldn't lose me too. But Brian had made it clear that even if I gave him the money now and the drugs, he was going to kill me anyway. The only thing I could do was fight and hope I survived my wounds.

Right when I was about to reach for my gun, a loud bang on the door made us all whip our heads. Brian pulled out his pistol and aimed it at the door before gesturing for Gator to check it out. Gator crept to the door right as another loud knock came.

"Baby, it's me," a high-pitched woman said. "Open the door."

"Dammit, Tayla," Brian groaned and jerked his gun with an attitude. "Let that bitch in."

Gator opened the door, and a skimpily dressed woman stormed inside. She had an attitude all over her face, and her hand flew to her hip as she began talking fast.

"That little heffa out there keeps running off all my tricks. She keeps telling them I'm her mother, and she wants me off the street!"

"Wait, what?" Brian asked, confused. "What little heffa?"

"That *little heffa*," Tayla said, jabbing her finger at the open door.

To all of our surprise, Amber walked in. She quickly read the room, and her eyes went to the guns. She looked at me with worry in her eyes.

"You were taking too long," she said.

"Go back to the car, Amber."

"But why do they have guns out? Are they trying to kill you?"

"Aye, take this little bitch out of here, Tayla. Shoot her up with some drugs and dump her somewhere," Brian said.

"I'll kill you," I said.

"Motherfucka, you about to be dead, remember?" he asked and cocked his gun.

The sudden sound of a gunshot was so loud and shocking I was sure I had been hit in my chest. But I felt no pain. However, I heard Brian shout out in pain and drop his gun. Another shot rang out quickly after that, and I saw Gator fall to the ground in agony, clutching his knee. I looked at Tayla, who was running out of the room, and for good reason. I would be nervous too, if I saw a 12-year-old holding a smoking pistol.

There was a shocked look frozen on Amber's face as she shakily held the gun in her hands. It was still pointed at Gator, and I quickly took it from her and used it to hit Gator hard across the temple a few times. I didn't stop until blood splattered, and he was knocked out cold. I saw Brian go for his fallen gun, but my trigger finger was too quick for him. My bullet caught him in the shoulder, and he fell back. It was then that I noticed that Amber must have shot him in his hand. It had a huge gash, and blood was spilling all over the ground.

"Dawg?" Amber's soft voice answered.

"Go sit in the car, Amber."

"But, Dawg, I—"

"Now! You don't need to see this part."

She nodded and left the room. When she was gone, I glared down at Brian. He opened his mouth to say something else, but before he spoke, I put a bullet in it. His head snapped back, and he slumped to the ground. Gator was knocked out, and the bullet I put in his temple on my way out the door would ensure he'd sleep forever.

I ran out of the room and to the car. Amber was nervously sitting at the edge of her seat, waiting for me. I hopped in the driver's seat and sped off. As I drove, I didn't know what to say to Amber. Whatever big-brother image she had of me was now tainted in blood. She knew the real me now.

"I told you to stay in the car. And where did you get the gun?" I finally said.

"I told you that you were taking too long. And I took that gun from your room weeks ago. It was in your drawer," she said and crossed her arms. "You should be saying thank you."

I opened my mouth, and then quickly closed it. I wanted to chastise her about what a dangerous thing she had done and how she shouldn't have put herself in that position. But she was right. She saved my life.

"Thank you," I finally said. "And I'm sorry that your life will never be the same."

Chapter Six

Theo

A Rolls-Royce Phantom was waiting for me when I walked out of the law firm. It was mine, but I'd never sat in the driver's seat. Why, when I could relax in the backseat and get my mind together? My driver, Miss T, got out when she saw me approaching and hurried to open the back door. Everyone called her Miss T, but I just called her T.

"Thanks, T," I said and got in.

"Where to?" she asked once she was back inside the car.

"Razberry. My brothers should be there waiting for me."

She nodded and pulled away from the firm. Miss Tee had been working for me for a while, and she was fiercely loyal. My father was killed the same day as her son Trent. Trent not only ran drugs for my old man, but he was also his main shooter. However, a setup on my father led them both to be murdered. At Trent's funeral, Tee devoted the rest of her life to me. I'd lost a parent, and she'd lost a son. Her son was her breadwinner, and she desperately needed a job.

"I'll be your driver. And if shit goes down, I'll show you where Trent learned to shoot like that."

And indeed, she had. The worst thing anyone could do was let her aging face and petite stature fool them. Tee was a wolf, and I trusted her with my life. I got comfortable in my seat, and as I leaned my head back, I saw her staring at me in the rearview mirror.

"What?" I asked.

"How did everything go in there?" she asked, and I shrugged.

"Aw, that? Easy as pie. They're gon' get me off fa sho."

"Well, I still say what you did was foolish," she said, shaking her head. Yes, she worked for me, but one thing she would always do was speak her mind. "Shooting that sorry motherfucka and his ass ain't even dead was foolish. What you gon' do if he wakes up?"

"That's what I'm on my way to Razberry about. Him still having breath is the only thing that's testing my freedom. We gotta figure that out."

"If you was gonna put him down, you shoulda put him down," she said.

I heard her loud and clear. I wanted to snap at her and tell her to stay in her place, but she *was* in her place. Tee was the only one in my life who kept my head on a swivel because she wasn't scared of me, which was why I liked having her around me. She had the kind of eyes that told a story and had seen many things.

"I'll handle it," was all I said, and she nodded.

We rode in silence the rest of the way to Razberry. When we arrived, we saw the parking lot had many cars, which wasn't surprising. Razberry was popular for its late-night fun, but we still offered entertainment during the day and had a nice food menu. She parked in the back of the building, and I got out and went inside.

Razberry was what I like to call my pride and joy. Although my brothers played a big part in it, it was my idea. We had many businesses around town, but Razberry was what we called headquarters. It had an old-school player feel and the baddest dancers in the whole city. Although it was a public place, people who knew not to be there were never there. Over the years, my brothers and I had made a lot of enemies. It wasn't surprising since we were the kings of Atlanta's drug game. We had some competition, but they were ants to elephants. We'd put them down before and would continue putting them down.

I didn't hit the main floor of Razberry. I went straight to the second floor, where my office and my brothers' offices were. I wasn't surprised to see them chilling inside my office when I arrived. Cordell, a.k.a. Dell, was the brother under me, the middle child. He'd grown his hair out into long locs and liked to dress as if he were always going to a formal event. He always had a serious look about him, even when he was chilling. When I walked in, he was leaning back in a chair with his feet kicked up on my desk, talking to my baby brother, Myleek.

"Took you long enough," Dell said when I entered.

"Too long, apparently 'cause you seemed to have lost your damn mind," I said and pushed his feet off my desk.

He grinned sheepishly as I sat down to face them. Myleek was sitting in a corner chair looking unlike himself. He usually dressed impeccably like me, but today, he wore a white shirt with a big brown stain. He was the youngest, but he was sharp, which was one of the biggest reasons I let him in on the business when he came of age. Our dad had damn near bred Dell and me in the game. We weren't expected to be anything else but his protégés. However, with Leek, I wanted him to have a choice. After our dad was killed, I told him that if he wanted to go to school and make something shake out of that, I would be all right. Of course, he chose his birthright. And I couldn't blame him. The foundation and the money were already there. Plus, Leek could flip a brick faster than anyone I knew. He also didn't have a temper like me and Dell, which made him an asset. Knowing how to control his temperament was his superpower.

He noticed I was looking at his shirt and looked down at it too, before smiling. "I spilled some coffee on myself earlier."

"And you didn't change?" I asked.

"You told us to meet you here. I ain't have time to."

"Go in the closet and find you a different shirt to throw on. Lavys don't walk around dirty," I said, pointing to the closet door inside my office.

"This nigga," he said and smacked his lips, but he still got up and did what he was told.

"What's the word?" I asked, turning my attention back to Dell.

"Man, they got that motherfucka Michael on high watch. You'd think he was in witness protection."

"That's because he is. They're trying to hang my black ass out to dry, and he's their best bet," I said, feeling myself become angry all over again thinking about him.

"I told you we shouldn't have put that motherfucka on in the first place," Leek said, retaking his seat.

He'd found a black-and-white Balenciaga T-shirt in the closet and put it on. He shook his head at me, no doubt going back to the day I'd allowed Michael to begin pushing drugs for us. At the time, I felt it was a lucrative business move. He managed a different nightclub on the other side of town called Ocean. It was members-only and so high-end that even I couldn't get in there. Michael became my pipeline, and it was almost crazy how many keys of cocaine and pills he sold in a month. However, he'd started shortchanging me on my money. So when I told the Halloways that he had tried to rob me, I wasn't telling a lie. However, the nature of the robbery was fabricated. Michael hadn't broken into my home. I had invited him there. All he had to do was give me the money he'd stolen from me, and I would have let him go. I shook my head, thinking back to that night.

"You have a nice crib," Michael said, standing in the foyer of my house.

He'd come wearing his black work uniform and stood there with a smug smile. It took everything in me not to hit him one good time in the jaw for having the nerve to even be in a good mood. Over the last few months, I thought that maybe business had gone down for him at Ocean, and maybe people weren't frequenting the club. However, he was still selling out product every month and getting more. Yet, the money he brought back was getting lighter and lighter, which could only mean one thing.

"I would invite you to see the rest of it, but this ain't a normal house call," I told him, standing directly before him.

"If this is about this month's order, I plan on picking it up on time."

"Of course you are because how else would you steal from me without it?"

My voice was cold, and I studied his face for any change. His eyes twitched, and I saw his body grow stiff. Anyone else might not have noticed, but I did.

"Steal from you? I don't know what you're talking about. Why would I do something so stupid?"

"Because you're stupid, nigga. Motherfuckas like you don't know how to keep good business going. You get greedy and start skimming off the top."

"I—"

"Shut up, motherfucka. I'm not dumb. It might have taken me a while to catch on because I'm the one who brought you in, and I don't like admitting I made a stupid decision. But to my calculations, you owe me a hundred thousand. Where's my fuckin' money?"

"Look, Theo, I . . . I can explain. My son has medical needs, and insurance cut us off. I . . . I'll pay you back everything I took."

"Now."

"I can't do it now. I . . . I spent it already."

I snapped back to reality and continued shaking my head. It was the "I spent it already" that did it for me. There was no point in having someone I couldn't trust work off a debt. And if he didn't have the money right then and there, the only other form of payment I was willing to accept was his soul. I shot him in cold blood right there in my foyer. If I had known two close shots to the chest wouldn't take him out, I would have put two more into his dome. If he woke up, he'd sing like a bird, and I knew it. I'd done too much and gotten away with it for something so small to take me down.

"That nurse you be fucking with still work at the hospital?" I asked, and he nodded.

"She the one who been feeding me all my information. She said they have a cop watching him all hours of the day."

"Innocent until proven guilty, my ass," I said. "They clearly don't believe what I said, and him being unconscious is the only reason I still have my freedom. He gotta go."

"What we gon' do? 'Cause I can't lose you like we lost Dad," Leek said.

"You ain't gon' lose me 'cause this problem is about to be handled."

"What you got in mind?" Dell asked.

"You trust shorty?"

"Hell yeah. I wouldn't be fucking with her if I didn't."

"Good. Because I'm going to need her to do something for me."

Chapter Seven

Amber

I checked my watch when I pulled up to my brother's secret distribution warehouse that evening. Well, it wasn't really a secret warehouse, but Daddy didn't know about it, and he especially didn't know Dawg owned it. The functionality of the warehouse was legitimate since it was a loading and unloading spot for trucking companies all over Georgia. However, I knew that he used it for more than just that. It was the perfect business to move and get drugs delivered.

Finding out that my brother was a drug dealer probably would have shocked me if I hadn't already been shocked by the loss of my mother. I'd become so numb after that that I felt like a ghost in my own home. Of course, Daddy and Dawg were going through their own waves of emotions, so maybe they forgot about mine. Trying to navigate that alone was hard, and that was how my in-home adventures started. As I said, I felt like a ghost and wanted to see how much they couldn't see me. I found out so much about Daddy that I didn't know, like how he smoked cigarettes in his closet and hid them, along with an ashtray, in a shoe box. I also found the number to an online sex hotline. I didn't know if he ever called it, but I couldn't blame him if he did. Mom was always gone, and he was a man with needs.

It didn't take me long to start sneaking around Dawg's room too, and that was when things got interesting. To me, Dawg had always been a younger version of Daddy. Sometimes, I would jokingly call him the square out of all his friends. He was the one who had his head on straight and was going places, while his friends were the ones who were rough around the edges. Those thoughts faded away completely when I dug through his sock drawer and found a loaded gun inside. That finding alone sent me on a scavenger hunt through his entire room. And, boy, let me say, whatever I thought I knew about Dawg was all wrong. The drugs in the wall, large stashes of money . . . I didn't get it. We lived well and had everything we wanted and didn't want. So why was he selling drugs? I made it my mission to find out exactly who the hell he was, and then the night that changed my life happened. Not only did I shoot two people, but Dawg also killed them. I didn't see it, but I knew he did. He had to. Thinking back about it, I still couldn't believe I didn't need therapy. Anyone else might have cried like a baby, but I immediately accepted who my brother was. Nothing I did or said would change the path he'd chosen.

Dawg might never have known it, but he was why I chose to pursue who and what I wanted to be. It didn't matter what was already laid at my feet. I wanted to build a new road. And part of that new road included helping my brother whenever he needed me.

"Where the hell is he at?" I asked, looking around the parking lot as the last truck left for the day.

I didn't see his car anywhere, and it was going on seven o'clock. I was supposed to meet Leek outside the coffee shop in an hour. That day had been full of good news and surprises, but the main surprise was how Leek was lingering on my mind more than my meeting with Antonio. It had been a while since a man could even stay in my head for that long, but I couldn't stop thinking about how he looked at me. It was like he was staring directly into my soul, which sounded corny if I said it out loud, but it was the only way to describe his eyes on me.

I was about to call my brother and curse him out for having me come all that way when his car swerved in and parked next to mine. He got out wearing street clothes, which told me he must have gone home to change after leaving the office. I stepped out of my car too.

"I was about to call you and get on your head if you didn't show up soon. I have plans tonight," I told him, quickly hugging him.

"Plans? What kind of plans?" he asked with his brow slightly raised.

"The kind that isn't your business."

"Well, how important are these plans? Because I need you tonight."

"I thought you just needed me to meet you here."

"I also need you to make a drop for me," he said, and I groaned.

"Dawg, why are you always doing this shit?"

It might have sounded like I was mad that he wanted me to help distribute his drugs, but that wasn't the issue. The problem was that he always pulled me into his business at the last minute and completely disregarded the fact that I had my own life. I hated when he did that. But I understood why he needed me. Jimmy was the face of the operation; Dawg was the ghost. It had been well over a decade since Dawg had shown his face when making a deal. He never told me why, but I had a few educated guesses. He was the son of one of the most influential lawyers in Atlanta, not to mention a powerful lawyer himself. So, it was usually either Jimmy or someone else under Jimmy who would make every drop and pick up. However, there were times when no one else was available, and that's when Dawg needed me. The drop would always be in a place of Dawg's choosing, and he never let me go alone. He was always with me. I'd wear a mask since I too was the daughter of Darryl Halloway, and nothing could get linked back to him or the firm. It made perfect sense for Dawg to use me since I was a female, and nothing could trail back to him. We'd make the exchange of drugs for money, and we'd go on about our day.

"My bad. The burner phone pinged today. It's Larry Guzman. He wants to cop two tonight."

"Larry Guzman? Are you sure you don't want Jimmy to handle this one? What if he recognizes me?"

Larry was one of Daddy's clients, one who he'd saved from prison many times. He was a wealthy white man who couldn't quite keep his hands to himself when it came to the ladies. He was always getting accused of some sort of sexual harassment, and Daddy was always there to pull him from the fire. I'd never met him, but I'd seen him a few times when I dropped by the firm.

"Jimmy is busy handling other things, and it's an 'all-hands-on-deck' situation. And as far as recognizing you, he won't, but he for sure would recognize me or my voice. I've worked with him too many times."

"So, you won't be there with me this time?"

"Oh, I'm definitely gonna be there. I just won't be able to say a thing. Come on." He waved for me to follow him into the warehouse.

Once inside, he took me to his back office. When we were there, he shut the door and locked it. Although we were the only ones there, my brother was always cautious. He untucked his pistol and placed it on his desk before going to where a tall bookshelf covered the whole wall. There was a large red book of fables that our mother used to read to us when we were kids. However, it wasn't just a book. It was a lever. He pulled it, and a part of the bookshelf masterfully opened like a door. I wasn't shocked. I'd seen him open it many times, so much so that I stepped inside before him.

The secret room was put together like a small lounge, complete with a small bar and everything. However, it definitely wasn't a lounge. It was an artillery room with a wall full of guns and other weapons. On one of the couches was a bag full of fresh stacks of money, and on the ground beside it were a few duffle bags of drugs. He must have just gotten a shipment. I turned to him and shook my head.

"Why is all this just sitting here? You shoulda had Jimmy come move it."

"I told you, he's preoccupied at the moment."

"You've done too much over the years to be hidden to get caught up over some small stuff like this, Dawg. You need to move it."

"What, you my mom now?"

"No, but I'm the same girl who saved your butt all those years ago," I said, and he playfully rolled his eyes.

"Kid shoots two people and thinks you're in debt to them for the rest of your life."

"You are," I said smugly, and he laughed.

"Whatever."

"What's going on with Jimmy anyway? Everything good?"

"You know, ever since Jake died, Jimmy has been out for blood. The feud between him and the Lavy brothers is heating up, and bodies have been dropping."

"You said the feud between *him* and the Lavy brothers. You aren't involved, are you?"

"Of course I'm involved. That's my best friend. But I'm a businessman, not a thug. I'm in the game to make money and live to spend it. If he wants to continue to war, that's on him. But I understand why he's standing on business. Anybody would."

"Wait, Lavy? As in Theo Lavy, you and Daddy's client?" I asked incredulously, and he nodded.

"Yeah, I couldn't talk Pops out of representing him. The payday is too good. Jimmy doesn't know yet, but he will soon, and I'll deal with it then. Anyway, here. This bag is for you."

He went around the bar and grabbed a pink Louis Vuitton tote. He handed it to me, and I could feel that it had some weight to it. When I looked inside, I saw two bricks of cocaine wrapped in a scarf. Dawg then handed me an outfit with a pink Louis Vuitton skully to match the bag.

"What's this for? I mean, I get the mask, but what's with the outfit?"

"I booked a private dance class under the name Rain Hodges at 8:30. You won't be looked at funny for wearing a mask, but you still need to look like you're there to dance."

"If I do this, you owe me big time. I told you I had plans tonight," I said.

"And you still haven't said what kind of plans."

"The kind that involves going out with a friend and celebrating my painting being shown in Antonio Rondell's showcase this weekend," I told him and smiled.

My smile grew even wider when I saw my brother's eyes light up. His face was a mixture of happiness and pride. He gave me the biggest bear hug, and by how tightly he hugged me, I could tell he knew just how much it meant to me. I'd spent countless hours pouring myself into my work, which was finally paying off. When he finally let go of me, he was still grinning ear to ear.

"That's the dopest shit I've heard all day. Congratulations."

"You can congratulate me by making this all worth my while," I said before going into the bathroom in his office to change.

Chapter Eight

Jimmy

"Daddy! Oh, Daddy!"

The sexy squeals of a thick Puerto Rican woman filled my G-Wagon as she rode me in the front seat. I didn't know her name or anything about her other than the fact that she made my dick hard. I wanted her the second I saw her strolling the street in her tight, black, one-piece outfit. I didn't care what the price was. My hands squeezed her bottom, assisting in helping her bounce on my meat. I had one of her nipples in my mouth and was sucking it like a newborn baby. When I felt myself about to come, I grabbed a handful of her hair and yanked her head back to get a good look at the bitch who was making me feel so good.

"Yeah, take this dick," I said when I saw her face twisted into a pleasured pain expression. "Take this—aah, shit."

I felt the tip of my third leg tingle, and that was all she wrote. I came into the condom I was wearing, and by how I erupted, I just hoped that it didn't break inside of her. I didn't need any babies with anyone I didn't know and probably would never see again. Her pleasured look quickly turned into a smug expression when she climbed off me and went back to the passenger seat. While I caught my breath, she dug into her purse, took some wet wipes, and cleaned herself off. I looked down and was happy to see that the condom was still very much intact. I leaned up, took it off, and tossed it out the window. When she was dressed, she took it upon herself to reach over and wipe her remaining juices off of me with one of the cold wipes in her hand.

"Thanks, shorty," I said.

"No problem. You do know you have to pay for the full hour, right?" she said, and I looked at the dash in the wagon.

I'd picked her up and parked in an alley not too far from where she was strolling at about 8:15. It was now 8:30. I smiled sheepishly.

"Damn, shorty, that pussy got power. But I got you," I said, pulling out a stack of money. I peeled off five crisp hundreds and handed them to her. "The tip is included."

"Thanks, Papi," she beamed and started to get out.

"You don't want me to drop you back off?"

"No. You'll scare off my other clients. Even they know what I am, and none of us girls want to look like we *just* sucked some dick. Come back and visit me again," she said and winked.

When she shut the door, I started my Benz and backed out of the alley. Paying for pussy was more convenient for me than having an actual relationship. I didn't have time for women, but that didn't mean my dick didn't need to get wet from time to time. It paid to be the boss and to be able to afford any size and flavor I wanted, and then I could quickly get back to business. I checked my phone and saw a missed call from my cousin Mula.

"Yo," I said when I called him back, and he answered.

"Where you at, cuz? We in position."

"I'm on my way. I just had to make a quick pit stop. He there?"

The "he" I was referring to was Cordell Lavy. He was the middle child of a set of three boys, all three of whom were my sworn enemies. The day my brother was found dead, many witnesses said they saw Theo and Cordell speeding away from the scene. I wouldn't have thought anything of it if it had been anywhere else but my brother's trap house since Atlanta was so big. But Jake was so careful with his business, and the locations of his trap houses were so low-key. The Lavy brothers shouldn't have even known where they were, but somehow, they did. And that same day they were caught speeding away was the same day everyone in the house was murdered, including Jake, a.k.a. their biggest competition. Until I took over, that is. There was a snake somewhere in my grass, and I wanted to find it and cut off its head before the same thing that happened to my brother happened to me. But in the meantime, I wanted the Lavy brothers' heads on sticks. I wanted to knock them off their thrones, one by one.

What most didn't know about me was that I was cunning. Everyone, including my best friend, Dawg, thought I was just some hothead boss who only knew how to flip a brick. No, I was calculated too. See, Dawg didn't think I paid attention to details like he did. But I did. I had eyes everywhere, especially on the ones who took away my very first friend. I was shocked at first to learn that Theo was frequenting the Halloway firm after he caught a case. I was even more shocked that they'd taken him on as a client and represented him. Dawg and I had been friends for years, and I never thought he would cross me. I was sure he had his reasons for working for Theo, but as far as I was concerned, Theo could rot in the nastiest part of any prison. Eventually, that conversation between Dawg and me would be had, but it wasn't the time.

I'd learned that the man Theo had tried to kill was Michael Tony, but he was still alive, although unconscious in a hospital. That meant if and when he woke up, he could talk about what had happened to him. I didn't know why Theo had tried to kill him, but I knew for sure he wouldn't want him to talk. Which meant he would definitely be trying to finish the job. I knew because it was what I would do.

I figured out which hospital Michael was being held in and had it watched around the clock. I hoped it would be Theo I could catch slipping since he was the oldest brother and definitely called all the shots. However, when Cordell kept showing up at the hospital instead, I wasn't mad about it. He had some fine-ass RN who worked there. He often dropped her off and picked her up. It had been more consistent lately, and Mula could clock his moves. We'd been waiting for the right time to act, and that time had come.

"Yeah, he here. It look like he waiting for his bitch to come out."

"When he leaves, follow him. That motherfucka is dying tonight."

"Say less."

We disconnected the call, and I drove toward my childhood home. Jake had long since moved our mom out of the house, but he kept it around for business purposes. We were highly respected in the neighborhood. Everyone knew him, and everyone knew me. Not only that, but there was also no point in coming up if you didn't give back to the community that raised you. I tried my best to keep my brother's traditions going, like his food drives during the holidays and always making sure the elderly people in the neighborhood were straight. Every Christmas, he would get a big truck and load it with toys and gifts for the kids. Regardless of him being in the streets, my brother was a good dude, and he didn't deserve to die the way he did—all because of jealousy and greed. Jake could have knocked Theo off his throne if he wanted to, but he firmly believed that everyone could eat in the game as long as you knew your place in it. Toes only got stepped on if someone tried to come in your lane, and Jake stayed in his. I probably would never be able to live up to who he was because he wasn't done showing me the way. Now, all I was left with was a big hole in my heart and no guidance.

When I arrived at the house, I pulled to the back of it where Jake had a garage built. I pressed the remote in my Benz to lift the garage door and pulled in next to an old, beat-up Impala. Another thing my brother taught me was always to keep and switch out a throwaway vehicle. I never did any hit in my whip. That was one of the quickest ways to get caught up. Before getting out, I reached into the glove compartment and took out my pistol, a hat, and a pair of gloves. I put the gloves on my hands and the hat on my head. I didn't want any traffic cameras to see me just in case anything came back on the unregistered vehicle. However, I didn't plan on getting caught, and killing Cordell was just another black-on-black crime that the police would put at the bottom of their stack. I didn't plan on hiding my face when I killed Cordell. I wanted him to know exactly who sent him to the other side.

After I tucked the gun and put on my gloves, I got in the Impala and left the house, shutting the garage as I pulled off. The more I drove, the more I was excited to kill a Lavy. The bloodlust was growing with each mile I drove. My favorite time of the day was when the sun went down. There was no better feeling than being able to move around under the guise of darkness. No . . . There was no better feeling than *being* darkness.

Chapter Nine

Dawg

I almost laughed as I watched Amber twirling around in the mirror like we were really in the dance studio for a dance lesson. She almost looked like she knew what she was doing. The studio was a private one and expensive to rent, and I had to pay a costly last-minute booking fee. However, I'd pay any fee to remain in the shadows. Also, in an artistic setting like that, no one asked why we were wearing masks because many of the dancers wore masks as a form of being expressive with their craft. This was why I made sure Amber's matched her new purse. Details were everything.

I had requested not to have an instructor so Amber and I could have the room to ourselves. I sat in the back, posed as Amber's bodyguard while waiting for Larry to arrive. I checked my watch and saw that he was five minutes late. Then I took my burner phone out of my pocket and looked to see if I had any messages from him, and I, indeed, did. It said he was stuck in traffic and to give him ten minutes. I didn't respond and just put the phone back into my pocket,

"He's running late," I said, and she stopped dancing to turn and face me.

"Clearly," she said with her hands on her hips. "Are you *sure* he's even coming?"

"Positive. Larry is what I'd call a high-functioning fiend."

"Mmm," she said and sighed. "You know, Dawg, I've been thinking."

"About?"

"You. And this secret life you're living. When are you gonna stop? I can see Jimmy doing this shit, but you don't have to. I guess I've never asked you why you do it."

She was right. She never had asked me why. I always thought it was because she understood, but maybe it was because it was so crazy that she didn't try to until then.

"I do this for the same reason you create art—the freedom. My life was planned out for me the moment Ma popped me out. I never planned on following Pop's footsteps forever, but out of respect, I'm willing to do it for a little while longer."

"How do you plan on keeping this a secret for the rest of your life? He's going to find out sooner or later."

"Not when I move," I said flatly, and her eyes grew.

"You planning on leaving?" she asked, and I nodded.

"I want something of my own. There's not enough room here for me to grow. I never want to have a cap on the money I could make. To be quite frank, I could use the time I've been spending at the firm to expand my business dealings. I'm in a box here, Tink."

"Well, if you leave, I'm coming with you," she said, and I shook my head.

"You gotta stay and take care of Pops. He's already gonna lose his shit when I not only quit the firm but also stop practicing law. I'm tired of blurring the lines. It's time to pick a side."

"So, you're going to be a full-time kingpin?"

"The biggest. And then I won't have to be a ghost anymore. This shit has worked for as long as I've needed it to work for. Jimmy can have Atlanta. I'll go somewhere and start new," I said, nodding.

It was the first time I'd said my plans out loud. But it was all I was thinking about on the drive back home after meeting with Benny. I'd have to work out all the kinks as I went, but eventually, yes, I planned on starting my own operation. And I was taking Benny with me. I knew that could cause a rift between Jimmy and me. He would still have access to the best product, but I just didn't know how he would feel having to cop it directly from me. Not only that, but I also played a big part in his operation, so losing me would mean he would take a big hit. I hoped he would support me the same way I'd done him all these years, but Jimmy was a wild card, which was why I was playing it safe for the time being.

"Sorry I'm late," a voice suddenly boomed.

Amber and I whipped our heads toward the studio door and saw a stubby white man waddling toward us. Behind him stood two stocky men wearing suits and sunglasses. Larry didn't go anywhere without his bodyguards, which was a smart move because the guy was rolling in dough. And that was good for him because he had the face only a mother could love. I couldn't imagine how much pussy he had to buy even to smell it. He was a little younger than my father and had thinning blond hair. I stood closely behind Amber, holding the Louis Vuitton purse as he neared her. I watched his eyes travel all over her body, stopping at her eyes under the mask.

"Hello, Larry," Amber said, changing her cheerful tone to a low, businesslike one.

"You're the one I've been texting?" Larry asked and then looked at me. "Or was it you?"

"I'm the one who's talking right now, so what do you think?" Amber said, forcing his attention back on her.

"I was expecting Jimmy."

"Well, Jimmy sent me in his place. And you're late, and I hate when people are late."

"If I had known I was meeting such a beauty, I'd have been here early," he said, and although Amber *was* beautiful, he couldn't even see her face.

"Save the flattery for someone else. We're here for business. Next time, be early."

"Feisty, I like that," Larry said, flashing his teeth her way. "So, what do you got for me?"

Amber turned to me, and I handed her the bag. She pulled out one of the bricks and gave it to him. He tested it and nodded his head at the quality.

"Whew. Jimmy has the best coke I've ever had in my life. But I thought I asked for two," he said.

"It's in here, but I need my money first," Amber stated, and I was impressed with how good she was at acting like a real drug dealer.

"Of course." Larry turned to one of his bodyguards and motioned for them to step forward with the bag in their hands.

"Grab it, motherfucka," Amber demanded of me, and I almost hit her in the back of her head. When I hesitated, she turned to face me. "You slow or something? Grab it and count that shit so we can get the fuck outta here."

I fought the urge to laugh and did as I was told. I snatched the bag from Larry's guard and unzipped it. I quickly thumbed through the money to make sure they were, in fact, all hundreds with blue strips and then counted the stacks. It was all there. I nodded at Amber, who then turned back to face Larry.

"Nice doing business with you," she said, handing him the second key.

I put the money in her purse and handed them their bag. Once the transaction was over, it was time to go. One thing I didn't do was linger when I didn't have to. Amber and I began walking to the door, and I placed my hand on my hip just in case Larry tried to pull any funny business. He wasn't the type, but instincts were instincts.

***

"Grab it, motherfucka?" I asked when Amber and I were in the car and back on our way to the warehouse.

We were a safe enough distance away to remove our masks, and I couldn't hold back my laughter any longer.

"I was in the role, and you wanted me to be believable, didn't you?" she asked and laughed.

"Well, I almost broke character and hit you with that purse. One of them stacks is yours, by the way, and keep the purse."

"A whole stack? That's like $10,000. How am I gonna hide that much money from Daddy?"

"You're still on his account? It's time for you to grow up, baby sis," I said.

"I would have my own account if I had a real job." She smirked. "But thanks, I'll figure it out. And I *am* keeping the purse."

"The purse was yours anyway. Look at it as an early congratulations for selling your first painting. And aye, following your dream is a real job. Maybe you can take that money and get your own apartment."

She said nothing else, and I was sure it was because I sounded a little like Pops. When we got to the warehouse, I handed her the purse with the stack in it. I also offered to take her to get something to eat, but she shook her head.

"I'm going to see if it's too late to meet up with my friend. I love you. I'll call you tomorrow."

"I love you too."

I watched her get into her car and drive off before going into the warehouse to bag up the rest of the money. I sent Jimmy a quick message because Amber was right. It was time to move the product.

Chapter Ten

Jeffrey

There were a few smells that I absolutely hated, and one of them was hospitals. I almost gagged when I stepped through the revolving doors. It smelled like coffee and death, and then they had the nerve to throw some Lysol on top of it. Just terrible. I made my way to the receptionist's desk, where a woman with a curly updo was sitting and wearing a pair of scrubs. I tapped my freshly manicured nails on the countertop to get sister girl's attention, since she was all up into whatever she was looking at on her cell phone.

"Can I help you?"

"Yes, you may. When are visiting hours over?" I asked, and she checked the clock.

"You got about an hour left to see your loved ones. Who are you here to visit?"

"Michael Tony," I said, watching her look me up and down.

It was obvious that I was a gay man. I didn't even try to hide it in how I looked or in anything I did. I could see the question forming in her head, trying to figure out a way to let it out. Finally, she cleared her throat.

"And you are?"

"His cousin. You thought I was his lover?" I said and chuckled.

"N-no. I just—"

"Don't worry about it. What room is he in?"

"Unfortunately, Mr. Tony is under close police watch right now. Do you have any proof of relation?"

"Who walks around with proof of relation? Even if I had my birth certificate, it doesn't have my family tree on it."

"I'm sorry, I—"

"Look, my mama is confined to a wheelchair and couldn't make it up here to see her favorite nephew, so she wanted me to stop by. And wheelchair or not, that woman is strong. She'll kill me if I don't lay eyes on him. So please, just tell me what room he's in so I can calm her crazy ass down. I'll be in and out. Hell, his ass is unconscious. I'm not about to sit in there and talk to air for an hour."

She hesitated, and even I was impressed with how believable I sounded. My mama didn't even live in Atlanta, and Michael sure as hell wasn't my cousin. But I must have been convincing because she gave me a pass that went around my neck.

"He's in room 312 in Section C, so you'll need that pass to get through the doors. Take the elevator up to the third floor and make your first right."

"Thank you, honey."

I put the pass on and almost cringed at how the orange sat on my Bottega shirt. I followed her instructions and took the elevator up to the third floor. The moment I hit the first right, I saw a huge letter C on the wall and knew I was in the right direction. There was a locked door at the end of the short hallway. Beside it was a sensor that I held the badge in front of. Once the sensor flashed green, I could open the door and go through it.

It was very quiet on that side of the hospital, and as I walked past the receptionist's desk there, a woman gave me a kind smile. I nodded back at her and kept walking until I came across room 312. Sitting outside the door was a police officer who looked half-asleep. Nope. The closer I got, the more I realized he actually *was* asleep. I shook my head and breezed right on by him. I opened and shut the door to the room quietly and instantly heard the light sounds of a monitor beeping.

I studied Michael. It was a shame that he was in such a pickle. He was a handsome something even as he lay there with his eyes shut. I didn't know what kind of information Mr. Halloway wanted me to obtain, but one thing for sure was that I had the nose of a hound dog. Nosy was my middle name, honey. I moved around the room and began reading every piece of paper I could find. There was a notepad with some scribble on it left by his bed, and my eyes widened as I read it out loud.

"Patient Michael Tony stirred and opened his eyes this morning at 6:00 a.m."

He was conscious. I looked at him and almost jumped out of my socks when I saw him looking dead at me, wide awake. My hand shot to my chest, and I tried to calm my nerves.

"Who're you?" he asked in a low, raspy voice.

"I'm . . . I'm Jeffrey."

"I don't know you, Jeffrey. Who sent you?"

The way he asked the question made me look at the nurse call remote next to his bed. Slowly, I reached for it and moved it out of his reach. That motion made the questionable expression on his face turn to fear.

"Boy, ain't nobody here to hurt you, but I did have to lie to get up here, and I ain't going to jail in designer, understand?" I asked, pointing a finger at him. "Now, I'm here on behalf of Darryl Halloway."

"Who's Darryl Halloway?"

"What I tell you next, you have to promise not to alert anybody to this room, got it?" I asked, and he nodded. "He's Theo Lavy's lawyer."

I was prepared for it when Michael opened his mouth to shout. I placed my hand tightly over his mouth and gave him a death stare. The sound that came out of his mouth was barely audible. But still, I knew I had to talk fast.

"Theo doesn't know I'm here. Mr. Halloway agreed to take on his case without knowing everything that happened. And unlike most lawyers, Mr. Halloway has integrity. He doesn't want to defend a murderer, and he wants to know the truth about what happened that night. Theo says you tried to break in and rob him. So when I take my hand off your mouth, don't scream." I studied him, and after a moment, he slowly nodded.

My heart pounded when I finally took my hand from his mouth. But just in case he was lying to me, I was prepared to put my loafers to the test and book it out of there with no information for Mr. Halloway.

"Theo Lavy is a drug dealer."

"That's all speculation with no proof. We're talking about him shooting you."

"That's what I'm trying to tell you. Theo is a drug dealer. I know because he sold me drugs to push through the club I manage."

"Shit . . . This is big," I said. I knew how Mr. Halloway felt about drug dealers, and he would for sure drop Theo as a client once he found out that piece of information alone.

"He tried to kill me because I was skimming off the top."

"Well, that's stupid. He's a fucking drug dealer, so, of course he would try to kill you. Are you going to cooperate with the police?"

"If I do, he'll for sure kill me."

"Well, news flash, honey. He's probably going to try to kill you again anyway. I don't know much about that business, but I've watched a lot of movies. And you know too much. Your best bet is to work with the police and go into hiding."

At that point, I heard the door to the room open behind me, and I quickly stepped back from Michael's bed. I turned and saw a young nurse walk into the room. She was light skinned and had a fresh install in her hair. And, baby, she filled out her scrubs with her Coke bottle–shaped body. I didn't know why she would want to be a nurse when she should have been a model. Her name tag said Denesha, and she seemed shocked to see Michael awake, so much so that she didn't even acknowledge me. Her eyes were bigger than mine when I saw him looking at me, and if I wasn't mistaken, there was fear in her eyes.

"Mr. Tony, you're awake? How—I mean, when?"

"I'm not sure. But I'm alive, and if you're my nurse, I'm happy to be here still," he said.

I rolled my eyes. All men were the same. Michael was still on his deathbed, trying to get a piece of ass. The nurse gave him a nervous smile and then finally looked at me.

"Who are you?" she asked.

"I'm his cousin. I just stopped by to visit."

"Did he . . . say anything to you?" she asked, and I felt it was an odd question.

"Nothing much," I lied. "He just woke up when you came in."

"Okay," she said, relieved, and turned back to Michael. "Are you in any pain?"

"My chest hurts a little bit."

"I'll get you something for it and be right back."

Nurse Denesha left the room as quickly as she came, and I turned back to Michael.

"Remember what I said."

"What's going to happen now?"

"I don't know, but I'm sure Theo Lavy will be shopping for a new lawyer by morning. You'll be all right. There's an officer right outside your room."

I patted the bed once in farewell and left the hospital room. I walked the same way I came and was surprised to see Nurse Denesha on the phone in the hallway instead of getting Michael his medicine. She was speaking quickly in almost a frantic tone. I couldn't make out what she was saying, but I saw her nod and hang up. I wondered if the girl was on drugs or something. Nothing about the way she'd acted was normal. But that was her problem. I'd gotten the information I came for.

I stopped in the restroom in the hallway of section C. I was in there for about five minutes, but when I came out, I was almost bum-rushed by a trauma unit running down the hall.

I was confused when I saw them go straight to Michael's room just as Nurse Denesha walked out—not walking . . . *slinking* out. Like she wanted to be a fly on the wall. I hurried back to the room to see what had happened in such a short time. I looked inside and saw Michael lying there lifelessly as they tried to resuscitate him. It didn't work. He was dead. I walked away just as they called the time of death. But how? How had he died? He was just fine.

My eyes found Nurse Denesha again as she was leaving Section C. I didn't know why I did it, but as I said before, I was the nosiest person I knew.

So, I followed her.

Chapter Eleven

Cordell

"This girl needs to hurry the fuck up," I said, looking at the hospital doors and waiting for Nesha to come out.

It was the end of her shift, and I was there to pick her up like I'd been doing for a while. I didn't think I could fall for anyone, but she'd done the unthinkable: stolen my heart. It was pure coincidence that she was a nurse at the same hospital Michael Tony was put in, but it worked in our favor. We had eyes and ears on the inside. Michael's survival threatened not only Theo's freedom but all of ours. He was the seed that would lead back to our whole underground operation, and we couldn't have that.

At first, Theo wanted Nesha to keep a close eye on Michael just in case he woke up. But it was too much of a risk if he started talking as soon as his eyes opened. He needed to die first. He came up with a plan for her to secretly poison him in his sleep. What I hadn't counted on was getting the call that he woke up from his sleep while on my way to pick her up from work.

"Baby, what am I supposed to do?" she asked from the other end of the phone.

"Remember what we talked about?"

"Yes, but . . . but . . ."

"You scared? 'Cause I can't be with no scared bitch. This ain't just about life or death for Michael. This is about me too. If that motherfucka starts running his mouth, me and my brothers . . . It's over for us. And all the nice shit you're used to having 'cause of me? Gone. Understand?"

"I understand. It's just that there's a cop outside his door."

"And you a fuckin' nurse. Get in there and put that poison through his blood. You're the only one who can do it. Can I depend on you?"

"Baby, I—"

"*Can I depend on you?*" I asked again, trying to mask how annoyed I was growing with her by the second.

"Yes. Yes, you can. I'm gonna do it."

"I'm outside waiting for you. I love you, girl. You don't know just how much you're gonna be rewarded for this."

"I love you too, baby."

She disconnected the call, and when she did, I was left sitting there in the parking lot, squeezing my phone. The time had come for Nesha to show me she was a real ride or die. Some players in the game didn't involve their women in their lifestyle or let them spend their money. And usually, I was the same way. However, the situation at hand was an exceptional circumstance, and I needed her. The minutes that followed felt like torture, and I found myself looking at the clock. I was also prepared to hightail it out of there just in case she messed up, but I had faith that she wouldn't.

"Come on, come on," I found myself quietly urging.

When she finally emerged from the hospital, she was walking quickly, but not fast enough to alert any attention to her. She kept her head up, walked straight to the car, and got in.

"Is it done?" I asked but didn't even need to.

The look on her face said it all. She started taking quick, deep breaths as she nodded, and I took her hand in mine. I didn't care how tough someone was or if they didn't want to admit it, but that first body changed a person forever. Nesha would never be the same. But if I had to make her do it all over again, I would.

"I used an untraceable poison that made him go into cardiac arrest. He died quickly."

"You did good, baby," I said, kissing her hand. "You did good. Now, let's get out of here, and you know what else I was thinking? Maybe it's time for you to take a break from working. You don't need no job anyway. I got us."

"Promise?" she asked with grateful eyes on me.

"Hell yeah, I promise. After this, it's us 'til the end."

With that, I drove away from the hospital without looking back and called my brother to tell him the good news. The second I heard him answer the phone, a grin came to my face. They wouldn't have a choice but to drop the charges against him. It tasted like a sweet victory to me.

"What's up?" Theo said from the other side of the line.

"It's done," I said and began to laugh.

"Good . . . Good," was all he said, but I could hear the relief in his tone.

"After all this blows over, we need to celebrate. I'm thinking some tropical island shit," I said and grinned over at Nesha, who was beaming.

"I like the way you think. You really came through for me. I love you, man."

"I love you too. But me and shorty about to spend some quality time, and I'll—Oh, shit!"

I hadn't stopped at the red light on an empty street for more than five seconds when two cars pulled up on either side of me. On the right of me was an old, beat-up Chevy, and the other was a red Chrysler. I didn't care too much about the make and models because I was so focused on how quickly they'd just pulled up on me with their windows down. I recognized the driver of the Chevy as

Jimmy Falco because his face was uncovered . . . and that meant only one thing.

"Jimmy," I said out loud.

Instinct made me drop the phone to reach for my gun, but I wasn't fast enough. Jimmy's automatic handgun was pointed at my side of the car before I could even wrap my hand around the butt of my pistol. Beside me, Nesha started to scream, but her screams were cut short when the shots began ringing. My body was opened up by so many bullets, and I felt hot fire everywhere. When the gunfire stopped, I heard the sound of tires skirting off as I choked on my own blood. The whole car was blood red, and my body was rapidly giving out on me. I was still gasping for air when my head flopped to my chest, and my eyes went dim.

Chapter Twelve

Myleek

If it weren't for the tricks, Razberry wouldn't be the spot it was. After Theo spoke his peace about what he wanted to happen to Michael, I went back down to the main floor because that didn't really have anything to do with me. See, Theo liked to say Cordell was the hothead brother, but the truth was, in my opinion, they both had the same temperament. The only difference was how they chose to react in the situation. Cordell was a more emotional reactor, while Theo was more physical, which was why he was in his predicament. Our father would roll over in his grave if he knew his son had left a job unfinished like that. No, he would roll over in his grave knowing Theo let a scrub like Michael in on his business in the first place.

I was never green to the fact that I'd been born into a life of crime. Maybe my dad tried to hide it with Theo, but by the time I came along, nobody even thought to hide the drugs or the bodies. I was just expected to fall in line, which I did, and when I came of age, I joined the family business. My old man was one of the smartest businessmen alive and ran the show seamlessly. However, things began to change when he died, and the crown went to Theo. I loved my brother, but he was more obsessed with the power than really running the show. For example, he didn't care about paying the taxes for the businesses or tightening up distribution so that our trucks wouldn't get raided upon shipment. If it weren't for Cordell and me being responsible enough to seal the cracks, I was sure the Feds would have been knocking at our front door.

My father's drug operation had been so successful and foolproof because he paid attention to details. He was the reason why I was so thorough with everything I did. I didn't just look at something. I *saw* it. We owned many businesses, including restaurants, a clothing store in downtown Atlanta, and Razberry. Razberry was the only thing that interested Theo. He would rather have someone else manage the rest, and I wasn't for that, so I began making routine stops at the businesses. I'd never trust someone who wasn't a Lavy to take care of Lavy shit.

"You want a dance, Daddy?" I heard a seductive voice ask and snap me out of my thoughts.

I was sitting alone in a private section of the club, having a drink by myself, when I was approached by the thickest thing in the building. I turned to face her, and I couldn't lie and say the face didn't match the body. Her name was Vicious, and it was fitting because she *definitely* was vicious. From the blond weave, the shiny, plump lips, all the way to her pedicured toes. That night, she wore a leather getup that snatched her tiny waist and made her hips look even wider. The G-string she wore barely covered her fat kitty cat and got lost in her huge bottom.

When I didn't say anything, she took it upon herself to turn around and bend over. She began twerking for me. I watched her cheeks open and close, giving me the perfect view of her glistening kitty. I couldn't lie. I was tempted to rub all over it, but the thing was, I'd already had Vicious a few times. And the sex wasn't as good as she looked.

"Aye, you can chill," I said, pulling a couple of twenties from my pocket and putting them in her G-string. "It's real business on the floor. You don't gotta be in my face."

My words made her stop dancing immediately and whip around to face me. I could tell by the annoyed look on her face that she wasn't happy. She'd been trying to get with me since she started working at the club, but what she didn't understand was that pussy wasn't the way to my heart. That was everywhere. I could come to Razberry and have a different flavor every hour if I wanted, but that wasn't what I wanted. Of course, I was a man with urges and needs, but I preferred for my mind to be stimulated over my dick.

"Why you been playing me lately?" she asked with an attitude.

"Who's playing you? You at work shaking ass for the boss when you should be shaking ass for the tricks."

"You must got a bitch now or something 'cause you wasn't saying that all them times you had me bent over in the private rooms."

"Vicious, you know what it is between me and you. Nothing. I never led you to believe it was, either."

"So why you fuck me then?"

"You threw it, and it wasn't hard to catch," I said with a shrug. "I'm not tryin'a hurt your feelings, shorty, but it is what it is. You know what you're here for, and it ain't to be with me."

"But I wanna be with you," she whined and tried to press up on me.

She rubbed my face gently, but I removed her fingers. She wasn't getting the point. I hated when bitches acted clingy. Well, the ones I didn't want. It was a fact that there were some girls you took to bed and some you married. Vicious didn't even make it to the bed with me, and she for sure wouldn't make it down the aisle.

"Get that want out of your head. It's stupid. Get to work," I said and waved her away.

I went back to sipping my drink and heard her huff loudly before storming away. It was harsh, but I wasn't there to coddle anyone's feelings. But one thing Vicious had taught me was that it was stupid to play where you did business. Many beautiful women came to work at Razberry, but she was the last one who would ever sample my meat again. It was too messy. Plus, there was someone else on my mind. Amber.

I wasn't a sucker or a simp. It was rare that someone had me going off the first time meeting them. It was also rare that I had to make the first move. Humbly, I knew I was what girls called "fine as fuck." I barely ever had to do any work to get the attention of a beautiful woman. But Amber was prepared to walk right past me like I didn't even exist. Actually, she would have if she hadn't spilled that coffee on me. Not only that, but she also turned down my first advance, which never happened before. I'd heard since I was younger that men always wanted things they couldn't have, and I never took it too seriously. Mainly because I never thought there was anything I couldn't have. But now I understood the feeling. Not that it was a challenge, but it was intriguing to come across something new. I hadn't been able to get her out of my head since I'd seen her, which was why I stuck by her car.

I checked my watch for what felt like the fiftieth time and saw that it was nearing the time I asked her to meet me back at the coffee shop. Theo was still upstairs in his office, probably dabbling in some of the "merchandise," and Cordell had headed out to the hospital. I finished my drink and left Razberry before Theo could come and send me on a run for him too.

I drove my stealth-gray Corvette to the condo I owned in Buckhead, so I could shower and change my clothes.

I planned to take Amber to an Italian restaurant I liked called Zinos and then grab some kind of dessert afterward. I hoped she was as intriguing as I thought she was. It had been a while since I had anybody make me think. However, I truly felt she would live up to every thought I had about her. After all, she was meeting with Antonio Rondell, which alone was impressive. My father bought a few of his paintings as well as some from his showcases all around the world.

When I felt fly enough, I sprayed on some cologne and left to go to a store by my home and grab some flowers. I couldn't even remember the last time I bought a girl some flowers. I was always around hoes who didn't require you to be a traditional man. After getting the roses, I headed downtown to the coffee shop. I hoped she wasn't there waiting for me, but then, it was always a good thing to be fashionably late. I didn't want to look too thirsty. As I drove, my phone rang, and when I looked down, I saw it was Cordell.

"Hello?" I answered.

"Where you at?" he asked.

"On the way to meet this shorty. You at the hospital?"

"Almost there. I stopped and grabbed something to eat first."

"You sure Nesha gon' be able to pull that off?"

"She ain't got no choice. She my bitch, and if she thinks she gon' keep living this good without putting shit in the pot, she's out of her mind," he said, and I laughed.

"Nigga, you love that girl. She got you wide open. You pick her up, take her to work, and give her anything she wants. You ain't never did that behind a female before."

"Yeah, whatever. I still stand on what I said. That motherfucka Michael better be dead tonight."

"It shouldn't be her responsibility to handle that in the first place," I said, shaking my head as I drove. "Your brother is trippin'."

"Yeah? You tell him that."

"He don't listen to me. He only listens to himself. He's the reason we're all in this situation in the first place because he didn't think."

"Nah, he's in this situation because his neighbors heard them gunshots and sent the people to his door. He shoulda just made sure he killed that motherfucka."

"Michael shouldn't have been running drugs for us anyway. I don't care how rich the people are at that club. He never seemed solid to me. If it wasn't him stealing from us, it would have been him squealing on us. Theo just ain't like Dad, Dell. He's just not him."

"Ain't none of us like Dad. He was a rarity. But we all doing the best we can, and we need to have each other's backs. Especially with motherfuckas like Jimmy Falco running around."

I smacked my lips.

"Ain't nobody stunting Jimmy. He ain't made no real noise since y'all took his brother out all that time ago. He ain't doing nothing but racking up chump change."

"Nah, after doing something like that, you gotta keep your head on a swivel. Jimmy might not be the businessman his brother was, but he got the same kinda demon in him. I ain't gon' lie. If it weren't for Diamond, we probably wouldn't have been able to stick Jake's ass."

"Diamond? The one who used to work at Razberry, and they found her dead in that park?" I recalled.

"Hell yeah. Jake had started fucking with her on the low, and when Theo found out, he had her set him up. So many men's downfall is because of a bitch. She was sick about it, though, and she threatened to snitch me and Theo out. So, we did what we had to do with her ass too."

"Damn."

"I don't think anybody knows it was Theo and me, but shit, when you take out a boss like Jake, you can't put shit past nobody. But I just got to this hospital. I'ma hit you a little later. I love you, baby boy."

"I love you too, Dell."

We disconnected the phone when I was nearing the coffee shop. Cars were parked outside of it, but I didn't see the Range Rover in sight. I parked a little ways away and looked around to see if she maybe had done the same thing. But no, still no sign of her. I left the roses in the passenger seat and got out. At that moment, I felt foolish about not getting her number. I had been trying to be too player. Now, here I was, leaning on my car alone, looking up and down the sidewalk. It didn't take long for eight o'clock to come and go. I got back inside my car but didn't pull off right away in case she was running late.

"Nigga, you are tripping," I said out loud as I looked at myself in the mirror.

She'd clearly stood me up, and the reality of that alone was setting in. I looked over at the flowers and shook my head. I'd never been stood up before, and I didn't know how to feel about it. I wasn't mad or hurt, but I was disappointed because I really wanted to see Amber again. Once it was well past 8:30, I tucked my tail and started the car. I hated to admit it, but even as I drove off, I was looking in my rearview once again . . . just in case.

I headed back toward my condo, knowing I didn't want to be around the club scene that night. However, as I drove, my phone began to ring, and when I looked down, it was Theo. I quickly hit the silencing button and let the phone drop to my lap. I knew he was calling to see where I'd gone, and I wasn't going back to Razberry just because he wanted me to. Shortly after, my phone started ringing again, and when I looked, I saw Theo's name for the second time. I groaned and contemplated ignoring him again. I didn't, though.

"Hello?"

"Leek? Where you at?" Theo asked tearfully.

His voice made me sit up in my seat. I'd never heard him sound like that before in my life.

"I'm in the car. What's wrong?"

"It's Dell."

"What's wrong with Dell? I just got off the phone with him like an hour ago."

"He dead. He dead, Leek."

"What? Nah . . . I *just* got off the phone with him not too long ago." I shook my head in denial.

"I'm telling you, I heard it . . . We was on the phone too. And they just found his body in the whip. He gone, Leek. He gone."

I swerved to the side of the road and parked, trying to let Theo's words register. Dell was dead? My brother was gone? It couldn't be real. How?

"What happened? A wreck?" I asked.

"No. They shot up the car. Him and his bitch is dead," he said, and it felt like a dagger had gone right through my heart.

"Who shot the car up?" I asked, feeling the sadness in me turn to anger. "Who the fuck killed my brother?"

"I don't know. But I heard him say Jimmy's name right before I heard all the shots. They did him dirty, Leek. He ain't have a chance."

"Jimmy?" I asked, thinking back to my last conversation with Dell. "Jimmy did this?"

"I don't know, but we gon' find out. Right now, we gotta go to the morgue and identify him. I'll send the addy. And, Leek, I don't want you going nowhere alone no more. Keep a couple of niggas with you until we get this sorted out."

"I'll be a'ight. I got my pole, and my head gon' be on a swivel. I'll see you in a second."

When I hung up, I just sat in disbelief for a few moments. I stared at the steering wheel as the sounds of cars whizzing past me faded away. Everything was a blur. My brother . . . dead? Flashes of our life together played in my mind like a compilation video, from us being kids to us growing up together. Hot tears streamed down my face, and I punched the steering wheel. I screamed through gritted teeth and tried my best to hold in the sobs forming in my chest.

"I'ma kill that nigga Jimmy. He's dead," I shouted out loud in the car before taking my car out of park and speeding back into traffic.

Chapter Thirteen

Darryl

It was unlike Jeffrey to be late for work, but here I was, sitting at my desk with no morning coffee and no paperwork to sort through. I'd called him multiple times but received no answer. I knew he liked to have a nice night out on the town from time to time, but even if he had to come to work hungover, he *always* made it in on time. I used my desk phone to try his cell again just as the door to my office burst open. I looked up to see an exasperated-looking Jeffrey stepping into my office. After shutting the door to my office, he began waving his hands in the air and shaking his head.

"What's the matter? Where have you been? You know I was supposed to review some documents for the Lavy case this morning."

"Mr. Halloway, after you hear about the night that I had, you are going to say to hell with that paperwork. And to hell with Theo Lavy."

"What did you find out?" He had my full attention now.

"On my way home last night, I decided to stop at the hospital and drop in on Michael Tony like you asked, right?"

"Right."

"And I had to do the most to get up in there, chile. They might as well call me a private eye. I was doing cartwheels and flipping and shit. I really need a raise."

"Jeffrey," I snapped, trying to get him back on topic.

"Sorry, Mr. Halloway. Anyways, tell me why the bastard woke up when I was there."

"He what?" I leaned up in my seat. "This might be the turning point in everything. What did he say."

"Basically, that Theo Lavy is a lying son of a bitch, and he did *not* break into his house to rob him."

"I knew something didn't sound right about his story. Shit, this might be the one case in history that I lose. Shit!" I hit my desk hard with my palm.

"Michael said the reason why Theo wanted him dead is because he *was* stealing from him. . . . He was stealing drug money."

"Drug money?"

"The rumors are true. Theo Lavy runs some sort of underground drug ring here in Atlanta, and Michael was pushing said drugs for him through the club he manages. The stupid ass got caught skimming money from the top, though. Apparently, Theo found out and tried to get him out of here."

"Well, I'll tell you what. There will never be a day in heaven or hell that I represent a dealer, especially one who manipulates and makes a fool out of me. Return his retainer and any other dime he's given the firm. He's dropped as a client. I hope what Michael has to say puts him under the jail."

"Michael's dead."

"*What?*" I looked at Jeffrey's serious expression as he nodded. I was glad I was already sitting down because too much information was coming at once. "How?"

"I don't know, but there was this nurse in the room with us, and she seemed nervous that he was up and talking. Like *really* nervous. When Michael coded, I saw her sneaking out the room, and something told me to follow her. I don't know why, but this is where shit gets sticky.

I still can't believe what I saw, Mr. Halloway, and I truly don't know what to do about it."

Jeffrey began pacing and fanning himself like he was about to faint. At first, I thought he was just being his extra self, but he genuinely looked disturbed. I stood up, grabbed him a bottle of water from my mini-fridge, and motioned for him to sit down. He did and gulped the water I gave him before inhaling deeply.

"She got in the car with a guy I've never seen before, and I followed them. I don't know why my ass is so damn nosy, but I couldn't shake the fact that she had something to do with Michael being dead. Maybe it was because I'd just talked to him. I don't know. Either way, I followed them . . . and . . ."

"And *what*, Jeffrey?" I urged him to go on.

"They stopped at a light ahead of the light I was stopped at. It all happened so fast, but two cars pulled on either side of it and shot it up."

"*What?*" I was almost in disbelief. The story sounded like something out of an old hood movie. "Shot it up?"

"Mr. Halloway," Jeffrey said, looking me in my eyes. "They. *Shot. It. Up.* That car had so many holes in it, it looked like Swiss cheese."

"So, the nurse kills Michael, you think, and then someone comes and kills the nurse. But who would do something like that?"

"It was Jimmy, Mr. Halloway. I saw him in one of the cars when it turned in front of me to get on the side of them. It was Jimmy. *He* killed them."

"Jimmy, Dawg's best friend, Jimmy?" I asked, and he nodded.

"I don't know what kind of shit he's in, but it was definitely him."

Jimmy and Dawg had been close for years. It was a friendship that sometimes didn't make sense to me, given the fact that the two boys came from entirely different backgrounds. True, they both went to the same private school, but Jimmy's home life was sketchy. I knew he had an older brother who ran the streets and eventually got murdered in them, but I didn't know that Jimmy had followed in his footsteps. It made me wonder about my own son and how much he knew about his so-called best friend.

At that moment, someone knocked loudly on my office door, and then once again. It swung open before I could tell the person to enter. My son rushed in, and before he could open his mouth, he furrowed his brow and looked from Jeffrey to me.

"What's wrong?" he asked, reading the room.

"Nothing, nothing," I said quickly. "What do you need?"

"Cordell Lavy, Theo's younger brother? He's dead. He was found in a car with his girlfriend late last night, shot to death."

My jaw almost hit the floor, and Jeffrey's hand flew to his mouth to hide his gasp. All I could do was pull my cell phone out of my pocket and check the news. Sure enough, Cordell Lavy's photo, along with a young lady's, was posted on every major blog site in Atlanta. The killing was going viral, and soon, the world would know about what happened. I had more questions than answers, and I needed those answers.

Not only that, but what was Jimmy's involvement with the Lavy brothers? And why would he kill Theo's younger brother? I needed the puzzle pieces to fit together, and more so, I needed to know my son had nothing to do with it. Hindsight was always 20/20, and I was standing there looking at my son and thinking about how he didn't want us to represent Theo in the first place. Did Dawg know all along who he was?

"Jeffrey, please go do as I said and let Theo Lavy know the Halloway firm can no longer represent him," I instructed.

"Right away," Jeffrey said, leaving the room.

"Wait, we're dropping Theo as a client? What happened?" Dawg asked me, and I sighed.

"Let's just say I found out who he really is, and I can't stand by that."

"Who he really is?"

"A drug dealer, maybe even kingpin status. And now, his brother is getting murdered the same night Michael Tony dies—"

"Michael is dead?" he asked, and I nodded.

"It's too much bad publicity, and I want no part in it at all. I definitely want no part in anyone who is poisoning the community. Drug dealers are the worst kind of people. They destroy worlds, and they destroy families." I sighed.

"No, families destroy families. People indulge in what they want. If they can't control their habit, that's on them," Dawg said, and I was shocked at how serious he sounded. "Narcotics are only one kind of drug, but people are addicted to much more than drugs. Everyone has their vices, and we can't blame the providers of those vices for that."

I sighed, realizing then just how much energy I had lost in the last twenty minutes. I needed my coffee. I didn't respond to my son's statement. Instead, I patted him on the shoulder and went to the office door. "Theo might not be pleased about this, so let's prepare for any blowback."

Chapter Fourteen

Amber

Sunday couldn't come fast enough. I would be lying if I said I wasn't on pins and needles. My first art showcase. It was the moment that I'd dreamed of forever. Of course, I'd invited my father, but he was so wrapped up in his work that I didn't know if he would come. Regardless, I wouldn't let anyone or anything ruin my moment.

"Hold still," Lina said as I sat in front of my vanity.

She was behind me, trying to pin my hair into some elegant updo she wanted me to wear. I felt like my face had been stretched to capacity. Any tighter and my eyes would have made me look like I was Asian.

"Lina, do you hate me or something? Did I do something to you?" I asked as I winced.

"Oh, hush, Tink," she said with a laugh. "Beauty is pain, and pain is beauty. This is a big night, and I'll be damned if you go in there looking like some two-dollar tramp. You have to look classy. You have to *look* like an artist."

"I still don't see what would have been wrong with a flat iron."

"Boring. When you walk in, I want *all* eyes to be on you. I want them to follow you all the way to your painting, and only then should eyes leave you."

"You're so poetic. I love you," I said with a smile.

"And I love you too. Which is why I'm up here doing your hair and neglecting all my other duties."

"Please, you know you'd be somewhere hiding and watching your *Housewives* until Daddy got home from work."

"Aht! Don't you be blowing my cover. I deserve extra breaks sometimes."

I laughed because her breaks weren't just extra. Sometimes, they lasted all day. Daddy knew it too. He'd often caught her sleeping in his favorite chair in the living room or sitting on top of the dryer in the laundry room on her phone. But she'd been with us for so long, Daddy knew the house wouldn't function without her.

"Mmm. You're talking about classy. Are you sure I should wear that wine-colored dress? It's a little short, don't you think?"

Lina turned to look at the dress hanging on my closet door and smiled. The dress itself was stunning. It had a high neck and a unique design. However, it was short and even had a small slit on the left side. She shook her head.

"Just because you are classy doesn't mean you can't be sexy too. And who knows who you might meet there?" she said with a wink.

"Not this again, Lina," I said with an eye roll.

"Tink, when was the last time you went on a date?" she asked.

Her question triggered me to think of Leek. I'd tried to go to the coffee shop after helping Dawg, and even though there was hope in my belly, I knew he wouldn't be there waiting for me. And, of course, he wasn't. He probably thought I had played him. Who knew if I'd ever even see him again? If he was single, I couldn't see him being that way for long.

"I'm worried about my future right now. Especially since I don't intend to return to college like Daddy wants.

I have to focus on my craft one hundred percent. I don't have time for boys."

"Mmm-hmm. So you say."

"I mean . . ." I hesitated, thinking if I wanted to continue.

"What?"

"There was this guy I was supposed to meet the other night, but Dawg needed me," I told her with a careless shrug.

"Dawg?" she asked with an eye raised. "What did he need?"

"My help with something. No big deal. Are you almost done with my hair?" I quickly changed the subject before she could start asking too many questions.

She gave me a strange look through the mirror as she sprayed my bun with some hairspray to keep it in place. I avoided her eye contact because I hated lying to her. After she put a curl in my side bang, she stepped back to admire her work.

"Now, you're done. Do you like it?" she asked, and I studied myself.

My makeup was already done, and I couldn't lie. I looked like I could be someone famous. I didn't know who taught Lina how to do Black girl hair, but she did it effortlessly. Even my baby hairs were swooped to perfection. I grinned and nodded.

"It's perfect. Thank you, Lina," I said, getting up and hugging her.

I walked in my slippers and robe to grab my dress off its hanger so I could get dressed. The more I looked at the dress, the more I agreed with Lina. I was going to slay in it. She went to the door to leave, but right before she shut it, she looked at me.

"Tink?"

"Yeah?"

"I'm sorry I can't make it tonight. I know it's really important to you."

"It's okay, Lina. I know you're going to visit your family for the weekend."

"Okay, honey. And, Tink, be careful, okay?"

"Tonight? I'll be okay. I'm sure there will be security. Dawg and Daddy might show up too."

"I'm not talking about tonight. I'm talking about your extracurricular activities. I've been in this house a long time. Your father might be blind to things, but I'm not. I love you."

Before I could ask her to elaborate, she was gone. Her words lingered over me. I couldn't help but wonder what she meant by them. Did she know about Dawg? Moreover, did she know about *my* involvement with him? Nah, she couldn't have. I finished getting dressed and touched up my lip gloss before leaving my room. I didn't even think of going to Daddy's room. I knew he wasn't home. I truly did hope he would think of popping up at the showcase, though.

After grabbing my painting, my heels stabbed the ground as I hurried out of the house and to my vehicle. Once inside, I placed my painting in the back seat and tossed my purse into the front seat before starting the Range Rover. I was supposed to get to the showcase early to set it up properly, but I knew I was cutting it close. I didn't think it had taken that long for Lina to do my hair, but then again, once we started running our mouths, that was all she wrote. I'd still get to the showcase early if I didn't run into traffic, but it was Atlanta. There was *always* traffic. I pulled away from the house and drove like my life depended on it.

As luck would have it, I did not get pulled over for reckless driving, and I also arrived at the showcase thirty minutes before the show started. The showcase was being held in a room inside the Atlanta Antique Museum, and when I got there, I pulled up to the valet. Before I was done grabbing my purse and the painting, a young white guy wearing a valet vest opened the door.

"Good evening, ma'am. May I?" he asked, holding his hand out for the key.

"Here you go," I said, handing him the key fob.

I got out of his way with my purse and painting in tow. The warm breeze hit my face as I walked inside the museum. I had to go through a metal detector, and a security guard had to check my purse, but, of course, I was all clear. I made my way to where the showcase would be and was in awe when I stepped into the large room. So many magnificent paintings were on display that I stopped walking to look around. I couldn't lie. At that moment, I felt small. How could I compete with so much greatness? How would *my* painting stand out in a room full of unicorns?

"Breathe," I heard a voice say behind me.

I turned around and saw Antonio approaching me, looking like a gust of fresh air. He had a slight smile frozen on his face when he stopped at my side. He gave a small, satisfied smile as he looked around the room.

"They're all so . . . amazing," I said.

"They are, and so is your work. So, breathe. This isn't a competition. It's more of a . . . compilation of overwhelming beauty. Come."

He began walking, and I followed him. We walked to the side of the room with an empty space on the wall. He pointed at the nail that protruded from it, and I knew to hang up my painting. When I did, I stepped back and felt like new life had just entered my body. I'd been staring at it since I finished it, but stepping back and seeing it against the cocaine-white wall alongside other spectacular pieces hit me differently.

"Wow."

"As I said, a compilation of overwhelming beauty. I make no mistakes. Now, I must go and prepare to welcome all my guests. As I've told the other artists who are showing here, don't hover over your own painting. Work the room. Enjoy the evening. I don't host these events just to put money in people's pockets. I want you to network and make connections. Make everything you can out of this opportunity."

"Thank you. Where are the other artists?" I asked, nodding.

"Most likely in the refreshment room. You are more than welcome to join them."

"Oh no, my nerves are too bad to put anything in my stomach. I'm okay, thank you."

"You'll do fine."

He gently touched my shoulder and smiled at me before he walked away. It was funny how nervous I was—especially given what I'd just done for Dawg days earlier. I guess that felt more like role-playing, and I got to be someone I wasn't. However, standing there as myself, I felt naked. I began walking around the room and staring at each painting, one by one. The depth some of them made me feel was uncanny. There was one that stopped me in my tracks. It was of many different faces put together, creating a unicorn with a black horn. Beside it was a portrait of a young woman created out of yarn. It was amazing that there were so many talented people in the world, which was why I wanted Daddy there to witness it. I wasn't an alien. There were others just like me. Maybe he would offer more support if he could just *see* and *exist* in my world for a moment or two.

"Which one is yours?" a deep voice said beside me, almost causing me to jump.

I looked to my right and saw a very handsome, tall guy standing there. He was dressed casually in a plaid shirt, jeans, and a beanie on his head. It was effortless, yet he wore it well. His brown skin was so smooth like butter, and his face was so defined and perfect it almost looked like he himself were drawn. He had one of those faces that would make a girl's heart sing, but his eyes? His eyes were a shade lighter than his skin, and I couldn't help but smile when they lay on me.

"I'm not sure if I should tell you," I said, and he smirked.

"And why not?"

"If you're an artist, you might try to sabotage my piece," I said half-jokingly.

"I'd never dream of doing something so terrible. I just thought someone as beautiful as you either created something even more ravishing or maybe you created something terrible." He winked at me.

"I wouldn't be here if it were terrible."

"Even terrible things can be art. Some of the ugliest paintings have been highly valued simply because of what they represent. Look at the *Mona Lisa*."

"Hmm . . . Which one is yours?" I asked.

"Oh, no. I'm not an artist. I just know the craft like the back of my hand. I guess you can say I was raised around it my whole life. My name is Jay. I'm Antonio's nephew," he said, holding out his hand.

"Cool. I'm Amber," I said, shaking it. "This is my first showcase. I'm sure you've been to a million of these if Antonio is your uncle."

"Tell me about it. I used to hate it until I realized the true value of the simplest piece. Respectfully, showcases like these are what have made me rich. I always buy a piece or two, and after the showcase goes viral, and Uncle

Antonio's showcases *always* go viral, I resell them at two and sometimes three times what I paid for them."

"You never keep them?"

"Sometimes . . . if they move me. I'm sure your piece will sell. It might even become part of the bid."

"Bid?" I asked curiously.

"Yeah. Some pieces are so popular that they have to be bid off instead of bought outright," he said as he checked his phone. "Excuse me, Amber, people have just started showing. I hope to see you when it's over?"

I nodded with a smile at his hopeful tone. He grinned back at me and left me standing there alone. Soon after he disappeared, the room started filling with people of all colors holding wineglasses. I quickly understood why Antonio had told me to work the room because it was easy to get swallowed in the crowd. However, I took his advice and forced myself to walk around and talk to people. For hours, I found myself in deep conversations about other people's artwork and expressing my own opinions about them. I constantly looked around, hoping to see Daddy or Dawg, but neither showed. Daddy was one thing, but Dawg not being there hurt me, especially when I always showed up for him.

Something in me refused to allow myself to be vain, so I stayed away from my own painting. I was an artist and was sensitive about my work. I didn't know if I could handle negative criticism about it. However, I was shocked when I finally glanced over at where it was hanging on the wall and saw a small crowd standing around it.

Suddenly, I *did* want to go over and see what they were saying about it. Why were they all standing there, looking at it like that? Did they like it? Did they hate it?

"You look nervous." A familiar voice interrupted my thoughts.

The smile that came to my face when I saw Leek holding a single rose behind me annoyed me. Because why was I so happy to see him? My stomach did a cartwheel as I took in him and his tailored suit. Ironically, it was the same color as my dress. However, there was a hard look on his face. Not like when I first met him. No . . . not hard. Troubled.

"What . . . What are you doing here?"

"I saw you meeting with Antonio Rondell and thought you might be here. Well, I hoped you would be here after I missed you the other day."

"About that, I'm sorry. Something came up. But wait, you know who Antonio Rondell is?"

"Girl, I might be a little rough around the edges, but I know my shit. I ain't no broke nigga," he said, and I smiled.

"I wouldn't think so in a thousand-dollar suit."

"Here, this is for you," he said, handing me the rose.

"Thank you," I said, taking it and studying his face some more. "Are you . . . Are you okay?"

"Truth is . . . I shouldn't even be here right now. I should be with my family. My brother died the other night," he said after a few moments, and I gasped.

"Then no, you shouldn't be here. Why *are* you here? Go be with them."

"I just needed something to clear my head, you know. And every time I tried to clear it, your face came to mind. So, here I am."

We stood there staring at each other for a few more moments. I didn't know whether to make him leave or hug him. I knew the feeling of loss too well. Being caught between mourning and still having to live your life was what created grief. I took his hand in mine.

"Can I show you my painting?"

He nodded, and I took him to where the small crowd was still formed. I pointed at it and looked at his face. He stared at it for a while, and his troubled expression softened. He left me to move to the front of the crowd. I would have lost sight of him if it weren't for his height. About ten minutes later, out of the corner of my eye, I saw Antonio resurface and walk toward me with the biggest smile.

"What?" I asked.

"Honey, yours went to the bid. It just sold for a hundred thousand dollars."

"What? A . . . hundred thousand?" I was in disbelief.

"Be proud of yourself. We have five minutes until the showcase is over. You did it, honey."

"Wait . . . Can I know who bought it?"

"That fine piece of chocolate right there," he said and pointed.

His finger went right to Leek, who turned and was facing me. I blinked back the tears as he stared through my soul. At that moment, I didn't even care that my family hadn't shown up for me because, in the end, someone special did.

Chapter Fifteen

Theo

It was a cold world we lived in, and the coldest day I ever felt was right then, watching my brother get lowered into the dirt in his casket. My little brother, man. It felt like our entire family came out to send him off. I stood stoic in my all-black suit with shades over my eyes beside my mama. Leek stood on the other side of her. She was standing there like a real OG, but I could feel her hand trembling in mine as we listened to the singing of one of our cousins. I heard her sniffle when they let the doves fly, and I squeezed her hand. To my surprise, she pulled it away and leaned more into Leek. That hurt me, but there were too many people around for me to react.

The funeral service itself had been short because Mama didn't want the pastor doing all that talking or trying to make an example out of my brother's death. She also wanted us all to come to the burial site before the repast at our family home. Once Dell was in the ground, everyone said their final goodbyes and threw their roses on the casket. Only Mama, Leek, and I remained when they were all done and walking back to their cars. Mama stepped forward first with her rose in her hand.

"Boy, you weren't supposed to leave me this soon. I don't want to believe that you're gone. I love you eternally, and I won't say goodbye. I'll see you again on the other side." She sniffled and tossed the flower down. When she turned back to face us, her eyes went to me. The stare she gave me was long and hard. It was almost a glare. "This is *your* fault."

"Mama, we ain't know this was gonna happen," Leek said, trying to defend me.

"Everything y'all do in them streets has a consequence. I know this ain't just some senseless act of violence. It was calculated, hich leads me to believe that y'all did something first."

"Mama—" I started, but she held up a hand to cut me off.

"I don't want to hear you lie to me, boy. Do you forget I was with your father for over thirty years? I know what comes with the game when you keep playing it. When is this gonna stop? Don't you know how heavy it was on my heart when your father was killed? Death is just going to keep knocking at my door until I have nothing left."

"Mama—" I tried again, but she put a finger in my face that time.

"Shut the fuck up. You want to be just like your father so bad, but you couldn't be him if there were *ten* of you. You don't have it in you, boy. Your father was in them streets to give us a better life when they put a cap on us and all our people. We had nice things, but he didn't care about being flashy like your stupid ass. He didn't start no street wars for no damn reason. You don't even take care of the businesses you need to wash that damn drug money correctly. Myleek is the one who had to do it and pay the back taxes on them."

"Leek does his part just like we all do. Dell knew the risks, Mama."

"The risks of a call *you* made, I'm sure. He probably was killed over your need to control this whole city. Stupid. Your father knew his place, and he was happy with it. Your hunger and thirst for power are going to be the end of this family. You done already got my baby killed. Is Leek next?"

She gave me the most disgusted look she could muster before she walked off to where Miss T was waiting by my car. Her words hit me square in the chest, and I stood there, clenching my teeth. She was right. It had been my call to kill Jake to get him out of my way. I'd seen him as a threat to business. My father was okay with making pennies in the game, but I wanted to go all the way. I wanted it all. And even with Dell dead, that didn't change anything. In fact, it made me want it more.

Leek placed a hand on my shoulder but didn't say anything. I shrugged his hand away and stepped up to the six-foot hole in the ground.

"Heaven or hell, I hope you're where I end up. I love you," I said and tossed the rose down. Then I turned to face Leek. "Give me your car keys."

"You ain't coming to the repast?" he asked.

"Nah. I got something I need to handle real quick. You ride with Mama and Miss T."

He didn't press the issue. He just reached into his pocket and handed over the keys to his car. We gave each other a quick embrace before I left him. I could feel Mama's eyes on me as I passed my own vehicle, where she sat in the back seat. I wish I could say that I was surprised by her disappointment in me, but I'd felt it for years. As I grew up, she used to call me her "problem child," and that was terrible. I was the oldest, knowing my brothers would follow me wherever I went. I didn't understand it, though. She was a hypocrite. How could she be mad at me for living the life she birthed me into? She constantly compared me to my father, like I was some sort of insult to his name. But the truth was, we were the same man no matter how we went about our business. We were both drug dealers, and we were both murderers.

I got in Leek's car and drove off without looking back. I didn't need another second of a tongue-lashing. I was a grown man, and even though it was a sad day, business had to go on. I was grateful that right before Dell had been killed, he'd gotten rid of my biggest problem.

However, there was still the pressing matter of Darryl Halloway. He'd sent me a resignation letter with all my money back, telling me that I needed to get a new lawyer. The only thing about that was he was reputable and had pull in Atlanta. No good lawyer would touch my case after he dropped me as a client. I'd called several of them. Most didn't even call me back. Although Michael was dead, I was sure the prosecution would try their best to implicate me for the murder if they found out he'd been poisoned. The nurse had been in the car with Dell when he got hit up, and that could possibly help or hurt my case. I was still in the middle of fighting, and I needed Darryl.

It was two o'clock in the afternoon as muscle memory guided me toward the Halloway firm. When I arrived, I whipped into the parking lot and didn't care that I took up two parking spots. There was only one other car there, probably because it was the weekend. I hoped that the Benz belonged to the person I wanted to see. Had it not been for the careless and callous way that I'd been dropped as a client, I might not have decided to pop up unannounced.

I exited the car and went to the front door, half expecting it to be locked, but it opened easily. The office looked the same as it always did when I'd visited Mr. Halloway, except there wasn't anyone at the front desk or bustling around the place. I went down the hall to Mr. Halloway's office and was happy to see that the door was slightly ajar and his light was on. I startled him by pushing the door open and closing it behind me. He'd been in the middle of going through some papers when I came in and stopped immediately.

"Theo, what are you doing here? We're closed."

"Apparently not. The door was open," I said and sat across from him.

He was quiet momentarily, and we started a staring match. I couldn't tell if it was fear in his eyes or pure disbelief that I'd shown up like that. Being unpredictable has always been one of my strong points. It kept my enemies on their toes. I was trying to figure out if he was my enemy.

"What do you want?" he finally asked.

"Come on, Mr. Halloway, you're a smart man. You know why I'm here. Take a wild guess."

"Can I assume it has something to do with the fact that the firm dropped you as a client?"

"I knew you could do it," I said, feigning a hand clap. "I wanna know what that was about. I spent a lot of time on my case with you, Mr. Halloway, for you to up and randomly discard me like trash."

"Unfortunately, the decision is final. All of your money has been sent back to you. I am sure you can find someone else to represent you," he said, and I laughed.

"You know you blackballed me. There isn't another lawyer willing to touch my case, and I want to know why you're moving like a snake, and you barely even know me."

"I don't know what you're talking about," he said, and it was his turn to have a slight smirk on his face. It angered me.

"I'm sure you don't. Listen, Mr. Halloway, I don't like being fucked over, especially by the people who I ask for help."

"Fucked over?" He gave me an incredulous look. "*You* don't like being fucked over? You know what? The truth is I *don't* know you. I don't know many of my clients personally, but when I ask them questions, I expect them to tell me the truth. Especially about who they really are."

"And what's that supposed to mean?" I asked, glaring at him.

"You know what it means, Theo. I don't represent drug dealers, and I don't represent murderers. Many lawyers will know their client is a killer and manipulate the system to make sure they walk free. And just like that, a killer is back out on the streets because he had the money to afford a good lawyer. You pulled the wool over my eyes, and I won't be known as a crook's lawyer. It's an insult to my name. I became a lawyer to improve the world and assist with injustices done to my fellow Black people. And unfortunately, I believe you are the worst kind of person."

"I'm not sure where you're getting your information about me from, but—"

"Michael Tony," he said.

"What about that thief?"

"One thing you should know about me, Theo, is that I'm not just good at what I do. I'm thorough. I have eyes and ears everywhere. And a pair of those eyes and ears were present for Michael Tony's return to the land of the living. And he had quite a lot to say about you."

"Like what?" I called his bluff.

"Like the fact that he ran drugs for you in his club. And the fact that you tried to murder him because he was skimming money from the top. But the funny thing is . . . not even five minutes later, Michael was dead. The cause remains unknown, but I think you know exactly what happened."

"How could I know? I wasn't there."

"But your brother was, and so was his girlfriend, who happened to be one of Michael's nurses that night . . . both of whom are now dead. Sorry for your loss, by the way. But if I could connect those dots, you don't think anyone else could?"

"Reasons why I need you to represent me and get ahead of this," I said, leaning forward in my seat. "I'm not going to prison, Mr. Halloway."

"Every dog has its day, Theo. I'm sorry, but there's nothing else I can do for you."

"I don't think you understand me, Mr. Halloway. Not only have you ruined my chances of having another lawyer as good as you represent me, but you also know too much. If you think I'm walking out of that door without getting what I came here for, you're sadly mistaken."

"That sounds like a threat, Theo."

"I don't make threats. I make things happen."

"I could call the police right now."

"And you'd be an even bigger fool. Even with me in a prison cell, you won't be untouchable. Neither will your family and everything else that you love. Now that the cat is out of the bag and you know what I'm capable of, we can have a better business relationship and understanding. I'll be kind, though, and give you until eight o'clock to make your final decision. But we know which one doesn't come with bodies dropping, right? I'll be back."

For the first time, he didn't have anything to say back to me. To me, that meant I'd gotten through to him. I got up to leave him to his thoughts. I always got what I wanted, and this time would be no different.

Chapter Sixteen

Dawg

Since we were no longer working on the Lavy case, I had a little more time on my hands to handle business. It was nearing eight o'clock, and I'd just pulled up to one of Jimmy's spots to drop off some loads. When I arrived, his cousin Mula was sitting outside on the porch, smoking a joint with John John and a few other of Jimmy's boys. John John was cooler than Mula, but he was a little too quiet for my taste because if you weren't talking, you were watching, which could be a good thing *and* a bad thing.

I hated it when they did stupid stuff like drink and smoke outside. It just made the house look hot. Mula and I were more business associates than friends. He and I were just like oil and vinegar, and the only thing that connected us was Jimmy. Mula was a shooter. He wasn't a hothead, but he moved too quickly. He acted first and thought about the repercussions of his actions way after the fact. He gave me a silent nod as I passed him, holding the bags.

"You good?" I asked.

"Why wouldn't I be?"

"Because y'all out here doing stupid shit. Put that shit out."

Mula looked from the joint in his hands to the men around him. He started laughing, and they joined in. He took another puff and disrespectfully blew it in my direction.

"Nigga, who the fuck is you s'posed to be? The police?"

"Nah, but you moving like a fool ain't gonna do nothing but give them probable cause to search this place. And y'all shouldn't be kicking it out here anyway when there's work to be done. Why y'all chilling on the clock?"

"You s'posed to be my boss or something?" Mula looked around. "'Cause I don't see Jimmy nowhere in sight. So who the fuck is you talking to?"

I wanted to smack fire from his smug, doglike face, but I held strong. Like most people, Mula was one who didn't honestly know my place in the business, which was fine. It gave Jimmy leverage in the streets if everyone thought he was a one-man show. But the truth was, I was the only reason everyone ate the way they were. But the disrespect was coming to an all-time high, and there wasn't much more I was willing to take. When I said I held strong? I did it for about five seconds. Then instinct took over, and I snatched the joint from his lips and threw it on the ground before stepping on it.

"Yo, what the fuck?" Mula said, trying to stand up, but I shoved him back down so hard that his seat shook.

"Know your fuckin' place. There's money to be made, and you out here playing. That energy you just tried to give me? Use that to bag this shit up—now."

I tossed the bags in his lap, and he glared at me. After a moment, he gestured his head to the others, and they went inside to do as they were told. I shook my head. Power flexes came with respect, or they could come back and bite you in the rear. However, playing it cool for too long would make people think they could disrespect you on the regular. I would be happy once my own operation was up and running. The only thing I was missing was a partner.

"I thought you wasn't coming until tomorrow." Jimmy's voice sounded from behind me.

He'd just pulled up in his G-Wagon and was walking toward the door. I took notice of his disheveled clothes and the troubled expression on his face. My eyes eventually landed on a few droplets of blood on his shirt.

"I decided just to make the drop today. But fuck all that. What the fuck happened to you?" I asked and pointed at his clothes.

He looked down at himself and let out an exasperated sigh. "These hoes, man. One of 'em just tried to run off on me. Tried to take the whole stack out of my hands. I don't like putting my hands on women, but I had to tag that one. Fuckin' crazy bitch."

"I told you that you need to leave them hoes alone," I told him, laughing at the visual. "Them bitches are scandalous."

"Yeah, well, lesson learned," he said, shaking his head.

"Yeah, right. You'll be back tomorrow," I said, and he grinned.

After we slapped hands, he motioned for me to follow him inside the house. When I did, I looked around and made a face. Not only were there two half-naked women I'd never seen before passed out asleep on one of the couches, but also guns and money everywhere. I also took note of the lines of cocaine on the living room table. Mula and the others were in the back, doing what they were supposed to, but it was clear a party had been going on earlier. I looked at Jimmy to see his reaction, but he looked at his phone like nothing was wrong.

"Let me go grab this money for you," he said absentmindedly and briefly went back into one of the rooms. When he returned, I still stood in the same spot, and he laughed. "Damn, nigga, sit down. Relax or something. You want something to drink?"

"Nah, I don't want nothing to drink. I need to talk to you, though."

"What's good, bro?"

"The first thing is . . . Did you have something to do with Cordell's death?" I asked and studied his face. It remained emotionless.

"If I killed that motherfucka, you'd be the first to know."

"I'm just saying, you've been wanting to get back at them for what happened to Jake for years. I would just find it strange if you didn't tell me," I said, and he made a face.

"I didn't know I needed to check in with you about every move I made."

"You do when it affects business and can come back to me, especially if you aren't being smart. Like this crib. What's going on in here?" I asked and motioned around me.

"What you mean?" Jimmy asked, looking around, trying to figure out what I was talking about.

"Them." I pointed at the sleeping women, and he grinned.

"Aww, them just the house bitches. They help up bag shit, count the money, and keep these niggas' dicks wet when they're too uptight. Ain't nothing like working with a released sack, feel me?"

"I don't. Who are they? They could be working with the Feds for all you know. And all this shit." I motioned around the room. "This ain't smooth, bro. And I don't give a fuck if these are your people. If they're using, that means they're buying. Why is all this money and product out? And the guns, bro. What are you doing? One raid and everybody is going to jail. Benny would kill us if he knew this was how flawed we were moving. We a direct tie back to him."

I watched Jimmy stiffen, which was something he'd done since we were kids when he didn't like something he was hearing. Not only that, but he also hated being told he was wrong or being told what to do. But I'd be a fool not to let him know he was moving sloppy.

He took a breath but nodded his head. "You right, Dawg. This ain't smooth. I'm trippin'. I'll get rid of the bitches and switch spots first thing next week."

"A'ight, good," I said and prepared to leave.

"Aye, Dawg. Quick question, though. Since we're on the topic of moving flawed, when you was gon' tell me that you and your pops was representing Theo Lavy?"

"It's not even like that, Jimmy." I sighed. I knew it was coming.

"Then what *is* it like? You representing the motherfucka who killed Jake, bro. That ain't smooth."

"I tried to talk Pops out of it, but you know he don't know the extras about my life. I had to make a decision, and I ain't know how you'd take it."

"Badly, nigga. That nigga can rot under a jail cell for all I care. One less Lavy to worry about," he said angrily, and I understood because I would feel the same way if someone hurt Amber.

"Look, if it makes you feel any better, Pops dropped him as a client. You know how he feels about drug dealers, and he found out about Theo somehow. So he wants no dealings with him and his dirty money."

"So, how you think he gon' feel when he finds out his perfect son is just as dirty?" Jimmy said with a sly smirk.

The way he said it made my skin crawl. There would be a day when my father discovered exactly who I was. I knew it would break his heart, and he would want to disown me. But that time would be a long time down the road, hopefully. And by then, maybe he would respect me enough to stand by my side.

"I'll get up with you later," was all I said to Jimmy before leaving the house with the bag of money he'd given me.

What Jimmy didn't know was the money in the bag was the last of what I needed to cop a complete order from Benny by myself. It was time to boss up completely and entirely, and Jimmy needed to understand that he would have to tighten up if he wanted a supplier. It wasn't a choice. I knew now wasn't the right time to tell Jimmy about me relocating and starting up my own operation—or that I would be in control of *his* product flow.

I got in my car and drove away from the house to go stash the money until it was time to spend it. However, I was only halfway to my spot when my phone rang. I furrowed my brow when I saw Jeffrey's name.

"Hello?"

"Dawg. Dawg, where are you at?" he asked in a hushed and hurried tone.

"I'm just out running some errands. Everything good?"

"You need to get to the firm right away. It's your father. He's . . . he's—"

"He's what? Does he need me for something?"

"No, honey. Oh, Dawg, I don't know how to say this. Mr. Halloway . . . Mr. Halloway is *dead*. He's been killed."

Act Two

Chapter Seventeen

Amber

"Amazing grace, how sweet the sound that saved a wretch like me. I once was lost, but now I'm found. Was blind, but now I see."

Numb. Lost. Confused. Those were the only words to describe how I felt standing there in front of Old Baptist Church, looking at a casket that held my father's body. It didn't even feel real. Because how could it be? Parents were supposed to die before their children, but not like that, and not so suddenly. But there I was, going through the same thing twice. Both of my parents had been stolen from me, and now, I was an orphan. Both my brother and I were.

If it weren't for Dawg's strong arm around the back of my shoulders and Lina's hand squeezing mine in hers, I would have already dropped to my knees. But they were holding me up, and I knew that was the only thing holding *them* up. Jeffrey stood on the other side of Dawg, wearing a veil over his face, but I could tell by the way his shoulders were shaking that he was bawling and didn't want us to see. I wished I could offer him comfort, but I didn't even have any to give myself. My face was blank but completely drenched with tears. Receiving the news that my father had been killed in his office, I had so many questions. Why? When? Who?

The service wasn't long, but it seemed to last a lifetime. I knew I'd never remember all the faces who came and offered condolences at the repast because all I was thinking about was my father's casket being lowered into the ground. He was gone. I didn't know when the reality of it would set in. The day passed like a blur, and before I knew it, I was back home, still wearing my black dress, curled up in my bed in Lina's arms. It was then and only then that I let my sobbing be heard. Lina held me tightly, and I felt her own tears dropping on my forehead as we rocked slowly together.

"How did this happen?" I asked hoarsely. "Who would kill Daddy?"

"I don't know, honey. I don't know," she said, kissing my forehead and checking the time on the clock. "We *will* get through this, but first, there is something we must do."

"No." I shook my head. "I'm not ready."

The executor of Daddy's estate was arriving soon to read Daddy's final wishes. I honestly wasn't ready because that made it final. However, I knew holding up the process would only hurt us all even more. So, even though I wanted to resist, I let Lina pull me out of bed, wipe my face, help me shower, and get changed the same way she had when I was a little girl. My eyes were still a little puffy, but I felt a little better. She led me downstairs to the living room, and when we got there, Dawg was already seated there, waiting.

He was still in his suit from the funeral service earlier that day and looked as if he hadn't slept a wink. I sat beside him, and Lina sat in a chair beside us. She took a deep breath and gave Dawg a stern look.

"I love you, boy, but I knew that one day your dealings would come back to haunt us all," she said, shocking both Dawg and me. "You think as often as I've cleaned this house top to bottom that I knew nothing about who you really are, Allun? I kept your secrets all these years because I knew they would break your father's heart. Now, I'll go to my own grave with regrets because maybe if I had said something sooner, this wouldn't have happened."

She said out loud the one thing no one else dared to. I couldn't say she was right because Daddy was a lawyer. He might have made some enemies on his journey, but I'd be lying if I said that the same thoughts as Lina's hadn't crossed my mind. But I refused to put that on Dawg's shoulders.

"That's not fair, Lina," I said, but Dawg stood up and kneeled in front of her. He took both of her shaking hands in his.

"I didn't have anything to do with this, but I swear I'm gonna find out and make them pay," he said in a deadly serious tone.

"You better," Lina told him just as there was a knock at the door.

She took her hands back and went to fetch the door. Dawg silently sat down next to me, but I could tell he was in deep thought. I knew Lina's words were weighing heavily on him. Lina returned to the living room with a tall Black man in tow a minute later. He was bald, with a Yosemite Sam beard, and wore a gray suit. In his hands, he held a long envelope.

"Allun, Amber, this is Albert Chapman, the executor of Mr. Halloway's estate," she said to us and motioned for Mr. Chapman to sit across from us. "Please sit."

"Thank you, ma'am," he said kindly and did as instructed. He focused his attention on Dawg and me with a sad smile. "First, I want to offer my deepest condolences. Your father was a hell of a man, and his passing has caused a ripple of sadness amongst all of our colleagues."

"Thank you," I said, and Dawg remained silent.

"That being said, there is still business that needs to be handled due to his unfortunate demise. Your father has a written will, and I will read it as follows. First, I will read what pertains to you, ma'am," Mr. Albert said, turning to Lina, who looked shocked.

"M-me?"

"Mr. Halloway spoke of you with nothing but fondness in his heart, so, yes, you. He wanted to be sure you knew that," he said, pulling out the first piece of paper from the envelope.

"To my dear Lina, life would never have been the same without you. You have not only offered me peace of mind all these years, but you have also become family. And family always takes care of family, so to you, I leave a sum of $300,000, all my vehicles, and the house that you have kept spotless and taken care of all these years. And I ask you to please continue watching over my children and supporting them in ways I may have failed to do so. You deserve more than I could ever give you. I love you, always."

"Oh, Mr. Halloway." Lina's hand went to her chest as Mr. Albert handed her the letter, two sets of car keys, and a small envelope that I assumed held a check.

I blinked back my tears as Mr. Albert pulled out another letter and focused on Dawg and me.

"To my two wonderful children, Allun and Amber, life with you has been one of my greatest blessings. Allun, you have always been a leader and the smartest in the room. When I look at you, I often used to see a reflection of myself, but now, I know you're your own man. One to be respected and valued. A king. No matter what, I am proud of you and pray you have light in any tunnel you choose. Know that I am always with you.

"To my beautiful Amber. Follow your heart, sweetheart. There is a reason why you are you, and I am me. And I'm sorry it took me so long to understand that. You will be great because you already are. I love you both endlessly, and there is no matter of time and space that will change that. I leave you both equal sums of $500,000 and whatever remains from my life insurance policy. I also leave full ownership of my law firm to you, with which you can do whatever you please. My dream was my dream, and I lived it. Now, it's time for you both to live yours."

When he finished speaking, I could barely make out anything in the room. There was too much water in my eyes. I wiped my tears away as he handed us both a copy of the letter and an envelope. I glanced at Dawg when he took his and saw a tear slide down his cheek. I reached over and wiped it away. He looked down at me, and I smiled. We were all we had now. We had to be strong.

"If you don't have any other questions for me, I'll be taking my leave now," Mr. Albert said and stood up.

"I'll walk you to the door," Lina said, guiding him out of the living room.

"You okay?" I asked Dawg when we were alone, and he shook his head. "We're gonna get through this, Dawg."

"I know, but there's something I gotta show you," he said, pulling out his phone.

"What?"

"Security footage from outside the firm the night Pops was killed."

"I thought the detectives said the footage from the firm was scrubbed by someone that day."

"They were, but I had my own cameras installed years ago that nobody knows about." He showed me his phone.

He pressed play on a video that was on the screen, and I could see a car pull in at about four o'clock the day my father was killed. A man got out and went inside. About thirty minutes later, he left.

"Who is that?"

"Theo Lavy. Pops thought he might be angry after dropping him as a client, but now we know just how angry. Look." He pulled up a second video.

That time, it showed the same car and man pulling up to the firm again at around eight o'clock. He went inside once more, but shortly after, he ran out, holding a gun in his hand. I watched as my heart hit the pit of my stomach.

"He killed Daddy?" I asked, and he nodded. "We need to go to the police with this, Dawg. He shouldn't be free if we have proof."

"No." Dawg shook his head. "Jail would be too kind of a place for a man like Theo. He has to really pay for what he did to Pops, and I'm not talking about with his freedom. I want his soul in the most painful way. And I need to ask you something, just this one last time."

"You don't even have to ask, Dawg. The answer is yes."

Chapter Eighteen

Dawg

I found myself stopping at our family house more often lately since the death of my father. I'd stopped going into the office and had turned over any case I was working on to the other lawyers in the firm. Amber and I hadn't decided what we would do with the firm yet, but I knew my time was done there.

I sat on my bed in the room I'd grown up in and looked around, trying to find the pieces of myself that had formed my current life. My eyes fell on all the pictures and posters on my bedroom wall, then traveled to all the sports trophies I'd collected over the years. I found my attention lingering on the books on my bookshelf, which sharpened my mind and assisted with my vocabulary. I even chuckled when I saw the large stack of *GQ* magazines under my nightstand that had inspired my style. Pops had gotten me a subscription, so, in his words, I wouldn't dress like a scrub and embarrass him.

My heart tugged, thinking how I would never hear his voice again. I couldn't remember the last time I had told him I loved him, even though I was sure he knew. It was heavy because I was now the head of the family, and I didn't know how to be that, especially since I was still figuring out my own life. The only thing that made sense to me was the thirst to get revenge on the one who took my loved one away from me.

Someone knocked at my door, and I looked up to see Amber standing there with a pink duffle bag on her shoulder. Her hair was pulled back into a ponytail, and her makeup was freshly done.

"I think I'm ready," she said, and once again, my heart tugged.

I was having second thoughts about the plan I'd devised to get even with Theo. Something about sending Amber into the lion's den made me uneasy, even though I knew she could handle herself. The only way I could think of to get close to Theo was with every man's kryptonite: a beautiful woman. I didn't know any other woman I trusted as much as I trusted Amber. The plan was for her to infiltrate his club, gain his trust, and then lure him to me. I'd handle the rest. She was 100 percent down with it, but if Theo caught wind of who she really was, I knew he wouldn't hesitate to end her life, and then I would be left with nobody.

"Are you sure you want to do this, Tink?" I asked.

"Hell yeah. I want Theo dead for what he did to Daddy. I won't be able to sleep at night until he's asleep forever," she said, and I nodded.

"I ain't pulling nobody else in on this. It's just me and you," I reminded her.

"And that's okay. This is a me-and-you problem," she reminded me.

She was right. As much as I would have liked the backup of Jimmy, I couldn't trust him on that mission. I truly believed he was the one responsible for Cordell Lavy's death, no matter how much he denied it. He was the only person I knew capable of pulling off such a hit, which meant he was liable to jump the gun and ruin it all if it went wrong. Theo had just as much firepower as Jimmy, if not more. Another reason I was uneasy was that I had to go out of town the same day Amber got the call back from Razberry. I wanted her to wait until I returned before going, but she insisted she would be okay.

"I get back in the morning, but just say the word, and I'll return like lightning."

"I doubt anything will go down tonight. I'm just getting acclimated. I'll be fine," she assured me and plopped down beside me. "The real question is, are *you* ready for Jimmy's wrath when you tell him you're going solo?"

"You think it's going to be wrath, or just him being upset?" I asked because it would be good to get an outside opinion.

"It's Jimmy we're talking about. The only reason he's okay with your position is because you are his connection to the plug. Technically, you *are* his plug because he can't cop from Benny without you. Right?"

"Right."

"All right, so then, if you're going half right now, how do you feel when he not only loses his other half but also has to spend it all, *and* he's going to be copping straight from you? Technically, that's you becoming his boss. I've known Jimmy as long as you have, and his temper isn't anything to play with. In his mind, he put you on, so how do you think he will feel knowing you surpassed him?"

"Damn," I said, analyzing her perspective in my head. "I knew he would feel a way, but I haven't thought about it in-depth like that. I still gotta tell him, though. I don't want him to find out from anyone else but me."

"Just be careful with that one. I know that's your best friend and all, but even your closest can turn into your enemy. I need to get ready to head out. I'll keep you posted."

"Aye," I said after she got up to leave. She turned to face me before leaving the room. I said, "Keep your pole on you at all times. The second you feel a weird vibe, get out of there. Don't try to be Supergirl."

"I know, Dawg, I know. You won't lose me too," she said, addressing my fear.

I stood up, walked over to her, and gave her a bear hug. Then I kissed her on her forehead and let her go without another word.

I stood there until I heard the front door open and close. I stayed in my room a little longer before it was time for me to catch my flight. I passed Lina in the laundry room on my way out the door. She and I hadn't really talked since her outburst at Pop's funeral. I tried to walk past, but she saw me and stopped loading the dryer.

"Dawg, *mi amor,* come here," she said and rushed out of the laundry room.

She wrapped her arms around me and rubbed my back. It was what she used to do to console me when my mother left to go out of town when I was little. No one but her knew how much it affected me not to have my mom around like the other kids. I kept it bottled up, but Lina knew. She would hold me and watch movies with me or read me stories. The only difference now was that I towered over her, and her head barely reached my chest. She looked up at me with sad eyes.

"I'm so sorry for how I spoke to you the other day. I was very upset. Losing your father has taken a toll on me. I wasn't prepared for it. I understand if you don't forgive me," she said.

"I'll always forgive you. We're family," I told her and saw tears instantly come to her eyes.

"Where are you going?" She pulled away.

"To make some life-changing decisions. I'm done at the firm."

"I figured you would be."

"I'm a drug dealer, Lina," I said to her out loud for the first time.

"I know that," she told me matter-of-factly.

"I've killed people."

"I'm sure that comes with the job."

"My life will get more dangerous because I'm taking it all the way."

"And if that's your decision, you better be the best there ever was, mi amor. And get some bulletproof windows for this house while you're at it. I trust you, and I won't judge you ever again, okay?"

"Okay." I turned away from her without saying another word, but as I walked, I felt a slight smile come to my face.

Chapter Nineteen

Myleek

"We hereby find the defendant not guilty of all charges."
 Those words weren't just music to my ears, but I could tell by Theo's triumphant smile he felt like he was on top of the world. He stood at the front of the courtroom in a navy blue suit next to his lawyer, a woman named Shelly Gray. She was a middle-aged white woman, but I think she was a shark in another lifetime. She had given the prosecution a run for their money and cross-examined all of their findings in front of Judge Paddox, one of the toughest judges in Atlanta. However, Shelly made it look as easy as eating breakfast, and I couldn't hide my happiness. I'd already lost one brother. I didn't want to lose another.
 Beside me, Mama had her arms crossed, and her lips pursed. She sighed, and when Theo looked back at us, she rolled her eyes and got out of her seat. Before I could stop her, she turned and left the courtroom. When I looked back at Theo, his smile had dropped, and disappointment was on his face.
 "All charges against Theo Lavy have been dismissed. Stay out of trouble, Mr. Lavy. I don't want to see you in my courtroom again," Judge Paddox said, and he hit his gavel on the stand.
 When he left the courtroom, I got up and went to my brother's side. We embraced, and I turned to Shelly with my hand out.

"Thank you so much for all you did for my family today," I told her, and she smiled at me.

"Don't thank me. I just do the job I'm paid to do. And I like to win, right or wrong." She winked at us as she gathered her things.

We walked out together, and once we were outside, she and Theo shook hands before she headed over to a set of steps to do a quick press conference. We watched her work the reporters like she owned them, so much so that nobody cared that Theo wasn't there to speak for himself.

"Do me a favor," Theo said as we watched her.

"Yeah?"

"Put her on retainer. I don't need any other lawyers with morals," he said as we started toward his car, where Miss T was waiting for us.

I knew he was referring to the last lawyer he had who dropped him as a client. One thing I could say about my brother was that he didn't take rejection too well. And I wasn't surprised when I heard about the man being murdered. I didn't ask, but I was sure Theo had something to do with it. It was something I planned to bring up because I didn't want him beating one murder case to have him thinking he was invincible.

"Where did Mama go?" he asked me when we got in the back of his car.

"She didn't say, but I'm sure she just returned home."

"She ain't even speak to me in there," he said, shaking his head.

"But she showed up, though," I reminded him.

"That don't mean shit if she's going to show the whole world how disappointed in me she is. I don't need that kind of support."

As I said, he didn't take rejection well at all, especially with it coming from his own mother. I couldn't speak for Mama, and their relationship wasn't my responsibility to mend. However, we did need to become a stronger family unit if we were to withstand anything else thrown our way.

"You know she's still mourning Dell."

"He's dead. That nigga is not coming back. She gotta get over that. *I'm* here," he shouted, surprising both Miss T and me.

I saw her furrow her brow as she looked at him through the rearview mirror. I too gave him a shocked look. He spoke about Dell as if he were nothing. Like he wasn't the reason he'd beat the charge in the first place.

"How do you get over losing a son? Chill on my brother, man," I said, unable to hold back the fact that what he said bothered me.

He whipped his head to face me, and I saw a blaze of fire in his eyes. However, he blinked, and just as quickly as it was there, it was gone. He sighed.

"My bad. I'm just tired from all this shit. I'm glad it's over, and we can get back to business. But speaking of Dell, you know I need you now more than ever, right? You gotta take over Dell's spot."

"I barely have time to do everything I already do. How am I gonna have time to distro too?"

"I don't know, but that's something you gotta figure out," he said dismissively.

"Why we ain't talking about getting get back on the motherfucka that killed Dell in the first place?"

"Nigga, you see how hot I am right now? Trust me, I got something up my sleeve, but now isn't the time to execute."

"How do you know Jimmy ain't gunning for you right now, this very moment?"

"Because if he's smart, he knows he's hot too. I guarantee he's been lying low. He won't make a move anytime soon, and I promise he won't be able to before I make mine."

"What do you have up your sleeve?"

"Just be ready when I call you," he said as his phone chimed. He glanced down and smiled big. "Well, I just got some more good news. We got some new merchandise at Razberry. I can't wait to test it out."

By "merchandise," I knew he was talking about the new girls starting that day. Although there were some house names, Theo made it a habit to keep most women on rotation . . . Out with the old and in with the new. I leaned back in my seat and didn't say anything else the rest of the drive to Razberry.

I got lost in my own train of thought. I didn't like how Theo was handling Dell's death. When he first heard the news, he seemed distraught. Now, it was like it was just a thing of the past. Everyone mourned differently, but Dell crossed my mind multiple times a day. It seemed like the only person on Theo's mind was Theo. I even had to push the thought out of my head that maybe he was only initially mad because he had lost someone to do his bidding. I hoped he wasn't that callous.

When we got to Razberry, I had plans to go straight to my office. He could go over the "merchandise" himself. However, once we were inside, he placed his arm around my shoulder and led me to the main floor with him. The club wasn't open yet, so the lights were bright, and the main floor was empty. He led us to a lounge chair facing the stage and waved one of the staff over to us once we were seated.

"Bring my brother and me a bottle of champagne. Also, go to the back and tell Vicious that we're ready to see the girls," he instructed.

The staff member nodded his head and left us. It didn't take long to get the bottle and our food. Soon after that, the lights around us dimmed, and I sighed, leaning back into the seat. I took out my phone and began to scroll on social media, hoping the process wouldn't take long. It depended on how many girls were trying to make the cut. Usually, there were at least ten. The lights hit the stage, and out came Vicious, wearing her usual sexy getup and super high heels. She smiled at us, showing her pearly whites.

"I've got something special in store for you two. And they all passed the smell test. You know we don't like funky bitches. Trust me when I say these girls are *fire*."

"I'll be the judge of that. Send the first one to the stage," Theos said, sipping his drink.

"Your wish is my command," she said with a wink.

She turned and swished off the stage as the music started playing. The first girl that came out was a petite white woman with a plump bottom and a pretty enough face. She came out and did a small routine before stepping down from the stage and sashaying over to us. She turned around so that we could have a good view of her body. Theo was very particular about the women he had at Razberry. He didn't like too many blemishes, and if a woman had had surgery, he didn't like scars at all. He seemed to like her because he nodded in approval.

"What's your name, baby girl?"

"Bunny," she said in a high-pitched voice.

"All right, Bunny, I like you. You can start tonight," he said, and she grinned.

She left and went to the back. The next girl came out, and it was the same process. Same with the next after that and the next after that. Before I knew it, over an hour had passed, and there was still one more girl left.

"I'm about to head out," I finally said to Theo when "Pony" by Ginuwine started playing.

I didn't know if he heard me, and I didn't care, either. I got up and walked away toward the stairs that led to the offices. However, before climbing them, something made me turn around and look at the stage. When I did, I stopped dead in my tracks once I saw who was on it, tearing it up. It was *her*. It was Amber. She was wearing a sexy lime-green two-piece, but nothing was see-through. She walked in her high heels like she'd been doing it all her life and even did a few pole tricks. Her focus was on Theo sitting in front of her, drooling like a dog. Hell, my mouth fell open slightly. From the first day I saw her, I knew her body was banging, but I didn't think it could do all that. Like the other girls, she stepped off the stage to approach Theo. To my surprise, he stood up and gave her a standing ovation.

"You are lovely. Mm-mm-mmm," he said, kissing her hand when she got to him. "And what do I call you, baby?"

"Star," she said with a giggle.

"Well, Star, you are truly that. These motherfuckas are gonna love your pretty ass. Can you start tonight?"

"Yes, I can."

"Perfect. Head on to the back, and Vicious will get you settled in, okay?"

"Thank you," she said with the prettiest smile I'd ever seen.

As she walked away, I watched my brother's gaze linger on her longer than it had on any other girl, and I knew what that meant. He wanted her. Gone were thoughts of going up to my office. I had to talk to her. Star, Amber, whatever her name was. I took the back hallway, hoping to catch her before she made it to the dressing room.

"Amber," I said right before she hit the corner.

She turned around, surprised at her name being called, but when she saw me, she was even more shocked. She looked down at herself and then up at me, and a small wave of embarrassment overcame her. When I got to her, I just couldn't help staring down into her eyes. What was she doing here? I would have never thought she'd be in a club like this one.

"Myleek?" she asked. "What are you doing here?"

"My family owns this place," I said, and she looked confused.

"Wait, I thought Theo Lavy was the owner."

"Theo is my older brother. This place was his idea, but it belongs to our family."

"So you're . . . You're a Lavy?"

"Is that a bad thing?" I asked, seeing the troubled look on her face.

"I . . . I—"

"New girl. Star or whatever, get in here so I can teach you the shit you need to know," Vicious yelled from around the corner.

"I gotta go, Leek," she said and tried to turn around, but I grabbed her hand.

"Amber, for real, what are you doing here? I thought you were an artist."

"Working, apparently now," she said defensively. "And I *am* an artist."

"So why are you here? I just bought your painting for a hundred thousand dollars."

"It has to go through Antonio's foundation first, which takes time. And even after that, money spends fast. You see how expensive my car is. So, this is what I will do to keep it flowing in."

"Look, you don't have to do this. I'll—"

"You'll what? Take care of me?" she asked, rolling her eyes and laughing. "You don't even know me."

"But I still spent a hundred thousand," I said and tried to plead with her using my eyes. "Please, I don't want to see these tricks touching all over you."

"Trust me, they won't. You won't either."

She pulled her hand away from mine and walked away. It didn't make sense. Why had she gone so cold on me? I felt played, but then again, she hadn't asked me to spend that money on her work. I'd done it because I believed in her, and she made me feel something. Granted, I hadn't seen or heard from her since that night, but still, I didn't think we were over. We hadn't even really begun. I wanted to kick myself because she probably just looked at me like a lick. I was no better than the tricks that frequented Razberry.

Chapter Twenty

Amber

I was so blinded by revenge that I would do anything to get back at Theo Lavy, even working at his club to get close enough to make him fall for me. Getting an "interview" wasn't hard, since Razberry was already looking for new girls. It wasn't a process we expected to take too long. I just needed to get him alone one good time so that Dawg and I could exact our revenge. What I hadn't expected was for Myleek to be there, or for him to tell me he was Theo's younger brother.

As I prepared for my first night at work, I felt like I couldn't breathe in the dressing room. I'd changed into a different pink outfit and put some jewels on my face. So many thoughts were racing through my head. If Leek was Theo's brother, that meant he was a drug dealer too. Now it made sense why he had so much money at his disposal to spend on my painting. But it also meant he was my brother's enemy too . . . which made him *my* enemy. Still, even knowing all that now, I couldn't shake the way his gaze made me feel when it was on me. I hated that he'd seen me in such a light because I wasn't an exotic dancer. I *was* an artist, but his brother had taken someone important from me, so I had to take his brother.

No matter how much I liked him. Leek was forbidden fruit, and whatever could have been between us couldn't be anymore. My loyalty was to my family, just like his loyalty had to be to his. I wished there was another way to go about things, but each led to Theo's death, and that was a fate I couldn't change.

I finished putting on my makeup and touched up my ponytail when the dancer named Vicious came up to my vanity station. She was pretty, but I could tell that she had a stank attitude. She must have been the OG dancer of the place because she acted as if she ran all the girls. She turned up her nose as she looked at me through the mirror.

"What were you and Myleek out there talking about?" she boldly asked, and I made a face.

"None of your business," I said and grabbed a garter to put around my leg.

She grabbed my shoulder and whipped me around in my chair, then got in my face. I could see the other girls sitting around me stop and tune into the drama. Vicious was so close to me that I could smell the mint on her tongue.

"Leek *is* my business," she said. "I'ma tell you like I tell every bitch that comes through here. He's off limits. He's *mine*. His dick is mine, and his attention is mine. Got it?"

"Yours?" I said with a laugh.

I wasn't expecting the hard smack she landed on my face. The blow was so hard it knocked my head to the side, and I could hear a few gasps, along with some snickers. I slowly turned my head back to face her and her smug expression.

"Like I said. *Mine*. Do you understand me?" she asked in a bosslike fashion.

I didn't know if she thought she was a pimp or what, but she had the right one that evening. If she thought I wasn't going to hand her the fake ass she was walking around with on a silver platter, she was utterly mistaken. I jumped up to give her the whooping she so badly wanted, but a muscular arm separated us before I could swing. It was Theo.

"Vicious, you must be out of your fucking mind hitting the merchandise like that," he said and tenderly cupped my chin to see if I had a bruise.

"She shouldn't have been talking shit," she said and smiled as she walked away.

Theo shook his head and focused all his attention on me. His gentleness didn't change the fact that I hated him with all my guts. If there weren't so many eyes, I would have taken the rattail comb on my vanity and shoved it in his neck. But I couldn't.

"You okay?" he asked, and it took everything in me to get back into character.

"Yeah, I'm good," I said.

"Okay. I just wanted to come back and personally tell you that if you need anything, anything at all, let me know, a'ight?" He gave me a small smile, and when he uncupped my chin, he let his thumb brush against my bottom lip.

It gave me the ick, but instead of gagging, I batted my eyelashes at him. I could see right then and there that it would be easy. I nodded my head and looked down, pretending to be shy.

"Thank you," I said in the sweetest voice I could muster. "And thank you for hooking me up with this job. I really needed the money."

"No doubt," he said and then whispered in my ear. "Meet me upstairs in my office after your shift so I can give you your hiring bonus."

He pulled away from me, and I nodded. When he left, I turned back to my vanity and looked at my face. My cheek was a little red from where Vicious hit me, but there wasn't a bruise. Still, I put a little more makeup on just in case. After putting on my shoes, it was time to go out and work the floor until it was time to go on stage. Walking out of the dressing room, I felt someone grab my hand.

"Girl, are you okay?" I turned to a pretty chocolate girl standing there, giving me a concerned look.

"I'm fine. It wasn't my first fight."

"Baby, that wasn't no fight. She slapped the shit out of you."

"And she's lucky I didn't do her as bad as what I wanted to do," I said, and she shook her head.

"Girl, don't do it. Vicious is protected up in here. That's why don't nobody fuck with her, and don't nobody fuck with Leek."

"Ain't nobody worried about that boy," I said, waving my hand.

"Keep it that way. The last girl who didn't stay away from him got sliced like Scar. Come on. I'll show you how to work the room. When you aren't on the stage, the key is to get the customers to buy drinks. You can also pick up a few *after-hours* clients that way, if you know what I mean." She gave me a knowing look, and I nodded in understanding.

I had no plans of becoming a full-blown exotic entertainer, and I for sure didn't plan on turning tricks for real like a prostitute. But I let her talk and acted like I was letting her teach me the game as I followed her to the main floor. When we got there, she took me to the bar to get a drink to calm my nerves.

"What's your name?" I asked.

"Lava, 'cause I'm hot as hell," she said with a grin. "What about you?"

"I'm Star. How long you been working here?"

"About five months. It's cool, and the money is great, but there are some things you need to know," she said, raising her brow.

"What?" I asked.

"I saw the way Theo looked at you. He wants you."

"That much is obvious, but why wouldn't he? I'm fine as hell."

"Just be careful, girl. Theo might seem like a sweet gentleman, but that man has a demon on him. Having his attention might seem like an honor, but once you let him hit, it's like he owns you." She got a faraway look in her eyes.

"Do you know that from . . . personal experience?" I couldn't help but ask, and she shook her head.

"No, but when I started—" She stopped talking to look around and make sure no one was close enough to hear us. Then she leaned closer to me. "When I first started, I came in with a group of girls recruited by Vicious. One of them was this shorty named Reesie. She was a cold-ass piece too, and Theo took a liking to her just like he did you tonight. She was so sweet but so naïve. He tricked on her and did everything any girl would want her man to do. She thought she was going to ride into the sunset with him."

"What happened to her?"

"One night, she called me from a hotel, crying and begging me to come get her. She said she had run away from Theo's place because he had beat her with a pistol real bad."

"Why would he do that?"

"I told you that motherfucka is crazy. She was on the phone, bawling her eyes out, terrified he was going to find her. She said he told her he had let her get too close and that she knew too much about his business. He said he couldn't trust her anymore and that it was time for her to go."

"Did you go get her?" I asked, and her eyes grew sad.

"By the time I arrived, there was already a coroner outside. She was dead. They claimed she was just another prostitute killed by a trick."

"Damn." I shook my head. "That won't be me."

"Look." She grabbed my wrist and squeezed it. "Just be careful fucking with him, okay?"

He needs to be careful fucking with me, I thought but didn't speak out loud. I just nodded, and we turned to the bartender. She ordered us a few Tequila Sunrises to loosen me up, but what she didn't know was that I was there on a mission. I didn't plan on working in the club longer than I had to. And if that night I could get close enough to Theo to lure him to Dawg's condo, then I would consider it a win.

Razberry was packed that night, and I spent most of it pandering to men on the floor and faking interest with a smile. Many men, women, and even couples wanted my attention. It was then that I was thankful my father hadn't plastered his children's faces all over because I knew what I was doing was a disgrace to his name, even though it was *for* him. I shook what my mama gave me enough times that I racked up $2,000 before I even went on stage. I had a small bag on my wrist where I kept all my money, and I couldn't lie. After the liquor set in, I started to really enjoy myself. The music and the vibes were right. Theo might have been a monster, but he didn't fool around when it came to security for the working girls.

I noticed Myleek was on the floor, watching my every move no matter where I was in the club. I'd been doing my best to avoid him at all costs, knowing I'd fold if his beautiful eyes gazed down into mine again, especially with the buzz I had. I kept telling myself to keep my eye on the prize. And finally, it was my turn to hit the stage. Like I'd done earlier, I went to the back and waited for my cue. The second I heard "I Luv Her" by GloRilla come on, I sexily walked through the curtains as the strobe lights hit me. I couldn't lie. I felt sexy as hell, and I didn't feel shy about showing it. I did a few basic pole tricks before sliding down to the floor and crawling to the edge of the stage. All eyes were on me as I worked, and soon, the stage was flooded with all sorts of bills. I found my target, Theo, in the crowd and locked eyes with him. He was eating up my performance, and I felt I was doing a good job making him think I was dancing just for him and everyone else were just spectators. I focused all my attention on Theo, which made me sick to my stomach because I could feel Leek's gaze on me too.

When my dance was over, I got up from the floor as the staff gathered all my money. The attention had me grinning from ear to ear, and I walked off the stage. As soon as I passed the curtains, I ran into Vicious, who was eyeing me enviously. I was sure she hoped our run-in would ruin my night, and I flashed her a smile to let her know it hadn't. She rolled her eyes at me, and I went to collect my money. I didn't care if it was a fake job. The money was very real.

I spent the rest of the night in the dressing room, counting how much money I made. The rule was to give 10 percent back to the club, which was fine because I'd made well over $5,000. When the night was over, and the club was closing, I gave Vicious my cut, put the rest in my bag, and prepared to meet Theo privately.

"Where you going? Oh, yeah. To go get fucked by Theo," she said loudly.

She laughed along with other girls in the dressing room. I rolled my eyes at them all and flicked off Vicious. She didn't know I'd turn her every way but loose. However, she would just be a waste of time.

My dance had sobered me up, and as I left the dressing room, I walked to the stairs that led to the upstairs offices. I didn't know which one was Theo's, but I was sure I'd find it. There was security all over, so I knew I couldn't kill Theo that night, but I was hoping to earn his trust so we could meet outside of the club. I didn't plan on sleeping with him, but I did plan on teasing him a little bit. I wanted to make him want more and then leave. I had some mace and two feet to run if he tried anything further.

As I wandered looking at the doors, I saw a closed one that said "Cordell." I continued down the hall, looking for one that said Theo's name, but suddenly, I felt a firm grasp on my arm. I was whisked around and met with my worst fear of the night: Myleek's eyes were staring into mine. There was so much disappointment in them as he looked down at me. He pulled me into what I assumed was his office and shut the door.

"Amber, what are you doing?" he asked. "I thought you was feeling me."

"Myleek, I can't do this right now. Plus, why do you care? You're fucking Vicious," I said and snatched away from him.

"I fucked her a couple of times, and that was before I met you. That girl ain't had this dick in months. I don't want her," he said, and I rolled my eyes. "For real, Amber. You feeling my brother?"

I wanted to tell him "yes" to make him leave me alone, but I couldn't lie to him. I couldn't hurt him like that because I wasn't. I didn't want Theo's body. I wanted to make his heart stop. But I couldn't tell him that, either. Instead, I just looked sadly up into his eyes.

"Leek . . . It's complicated."

"What's complicated? What, you need someone to help you? I'll do that. I don't want you in here," he said, pulling me close.

If there was ever a moment I felt like a Disney princess, that was it. They were the only ones I'd ever seen that got to fall in love at first sight. They were the only ones who got affection at their worst moments. And the way Leek's arms were around me, I felt . . . safe. I felt wanted. But why would he want me after what I'd done that night? I didn't get it.

"Leek . . ."

"Amber, I haven't been able to get you off my mind since the day I saw you. And tonight, all those men eyeing you down, I can't handle it. I ain't never felt this way before. I wanted to kill all of 'em."

"Leek, I—"

"Nah, I'm not fucking with this shit. And you ain't going to my brother's office. You're not, Amber. Do you hear me?"

I looked up at him and not only heard the seriousness in his tone, but I also saw it in his face. I nodded up at him and felt myself melt in his arms. I didn't know if it was the sudden throbbing between my legs or the fact that he was so damn fine that did it, but I couldn't help myself. I kissed him. The moment my lips pressed against his, I felt fireworks erupt all around me. The bag on my shoulder fell to the ground when he picked me up and plopped me on his desk. He made me lie back and took off my shorts. He spread my legs wide in the dimly lit room, but he had the perfect view of my shaved, glistening kitty. His sigh turned me on as he stared at it and licked his lips. I wasn't prepared for him to dive in face-first and give me the tongue-lashing of a lifetime. My cries were silent as he sucked my clit like a popsicle.

He was definitely skilled in the art of giving head because he made me come in minutes.

"Leek . . ." I moaned. "Leek?"

"Yes, baby?" he asked in between licks.

"I need your dick in me. In my mouth or my pussy. But I need it . . . right . . . now," I moaned.

He grinned up at me as he undid his pants and pulled out his thick monster. It was the perfect size, and I felt my walls contract just looking at it. I didn't need our first time to be romantic. I just wanted him to beat it up and make me remember it. For all I knew, it would be our first and only time. He opted to slide me to the end of the desk and tap the head on my sensitive clit, making me jerk at each point of contact.

"You can eat it another time," he said. "After this, you mine, though. You know that, right?"

I nodded. I didn't care. I would tell him anything to get him to slide inside of me. He placed the head at my opening and applied just enough pressure to get it through my tight hole. It had been a long time since I'd had sex, and my body was fiending. His lips found mine again as he forced his shaft all the way through. I moaned my pleasure into his mouth and made a face.

"Myleek," I moaned in bliss when he pulled out and thrust again. "Myleek."

He began to stroke it at the perfect pace, not too fast and not too slow. As he fucked me, I started to get so jealous that he'd slept with Vicious before me. There was no way a woman like her deserved to experience such a perfect man.

Eventually, Myleek had to push me back and climb on the desk to continue hitting it missionary, and truthfully, I didn't want to switch positions. My arms were wrapped around him, along with my legs, and I loved the feeling of him having his way with me. His hands fondled every part of my body as he pumped into me. We moaned together, and when his tongue wasn't down my throat, his lips and teeth nibbled on my erect nipples. I was so stimulated that my toes were in the air, curled. I didn't even care that my legs were getting tired. Putting them down wasn't an option. I didn't want him to exit the love tunnel, no matter how wet his desk became. I lost count of how many times he made me come. I just wanted another one and another one.

"I'm about to nut," he breathlessly said after what felt like whatever.

"No, please, keep fucking me. Please."

"I can't hold on no longer, baby. This shit is better than I thought. Fuck. Can I nut? Can I please nut?" He asked the question while diving deep, and my eyes rolled back.

"Yes," I moaned.

"Where you want me to nut at?"

"In my booty," I said freakily, and he looked down at me, surprised.

I kissed him, and the moment I felt him jerk, I pushed him up slightly and hurried to turn on my stomach. I opened my cheeks wide so he would have time to shove his hungry third leg inside my anus. He was able to get his tip inside before I felt him explode.

"Oh my God. I think I love you," he moaned and gripped my hips. "Amber. Oh, Amber. Fuck . . . Amber."

The way he was moaning my name with so much emotion was crazy to me. Was it because I was nasty or because he really liked me? He grabbed my chin from behind and lifted my head so he could sloppy kiss me while he finished emptying his load. He kissed my lips and all over my face, ending with three kisses to the forehead. It was then that I realized I couldn't hurt him by going after his brother in the way I wanted to. And for the first time in years, I would have to tell Dawg I'd failed at a mission. There just had to be another way.

Chapter Twenty-one

Dawg

It was early morning when I finally arrived in Florida, and to say I was tired was an understatement. I usually made the drive straight through in an eighteen-wheeler once a month. However, doing it twice a month definitely had me feeling it. I figured a compromise and a way to make the blow less harsh was to let Jimmy keep all the product in the last shipment and profit without paying me anything from it because it would cost him way more to re-up without me the next time. It was the olive branch I was willing to extend, and whether he wanted to accept it was his option. That, or find a new plug.

Before I got comfortable in bed, I couldn't stop thinking about Amber. I kept checking my phone for a 911 message from her, but there wasn't one. Instead, her messages told me that she had made it, was fine, and would talk to me in the morning. I was eager to know how her night went, but I could barely keep my eyes open. I set a few alarms to ensure I'd get up in the morning. The last thing I needed was to miss my meeting with Benny, knowing he was very busy, and I'd called for a second meeting within a month. After checking Amber's location and seeing that she was safe at home, I finally let sleep take hold.

***

"Son."

The voice was one that I'd been yearning to hear the most. It belonged to Pop and seemed to echo throughout my body. I opened my eyes, but suddenly, I wasn't in the bed at my hotel anymore. Instead, I was in a clearing on a bright, sunny day. What? Where was I? I spun around and almost jumped when I saw my father standing behind me. I stared at him, not believing he was actually there. He looked exactly the way I remembered him and, of course, was wearing a suit. It was navy blue, his favorite color. Before I knew it, my arms were around him, and I hugged him tighter than I'd ever held him before. I couldn't stop the tears from raining down my face. He hugged me back just as tightly, and he patted my cheek twice when we broke away.

"Hey, son."

"How are you here?" I asked incredulously.

"I'm not. You're dreaming," he said simply.

"So, this isn't real?" I asked, looking around.

"It's as real as you believe," he said with a shrug. "Come. Walk with me."

"Okay."

We began walking side by side through the clearing, which seemed to have no end. The air around us was still, and no animal or bug was in sight. There was just us. I kept looking at him, trying to take in even the smallest details of his face so I could hold onto them. He saw me looking and smiled.

"What?" he asked.

"I miss you. Amber and I both miss you."

"I never wanted to leave you. I don't think anyone is ever prepared to leave their children. But I'm at peace if you need to know. And I'm with your mother."

"Mama is here?" I asked and looked around.

"Yes, but not here," he said with a chuckle. "She'll visit you too. All you have to do is ask. But right now, there's a reason why you needed me tonight. You have a question for me?"

I didn't know what he meant until I dug deep inside of me. He was right. A question had been weighing on me. Maybe that was why he'd appeared.

"How did this happen?" I asked, and he stopped walking to look at me. I stopped in my tracks as well.

"I can't answer that fully, but what I can say is, it's not what you think. Bye, son."

Suddenly, everything around me started to fade. I tried to reach out and grab him, but my hand went straight through him. He gave me one last smile as he faded away.

"Wait! Pop! Don't go. Pop!"

I tried to reach out again, but he was gone, and I was all alone.

"Pop!" I shouted and lurched upright in the bed.

It took a few moments for reality to set in. I looked around the hotel room, and it came back to me where I was. In the background, I could suddenly hear the alarm clock on my phone buzzing like crazy, so I hit the stop button. As I wiped my hand down my face, it was hard to accept that it had all been a dream. However, Pops's words remained: *"It's not what you think."*

I tried to push it all to the back of my mind, seeing I only had a few hours to meet Benny. Throwing back the covers, I got out of bed and showered. The hot water felt great on my body like a much-needed cleanse. When I finished, I got out and wiped my hand across the mirror to get a good look at myself. If all went well, this would be the first day of the rest of my life.

After drying off and dressing, I sat down to call Amber before I left. She must have been reading my mind because her face popped up on my screen before I could hit the call button.

"Hello?" I answered.

"You good?" she asked.

"Yeah. How was your first night? I hate I wasn't there to cover you."

"Honestly, I'm glad you weren't there. I wouldn't want you to see me like that," she said, and I couldn't lie and say she was wrong.

"Any word on Theo?"

"He did exactly what we thought he would. It was too easy. But, Dawg?"

"What?"

"Dawg, I . . ." She hesitated.

"Tink, say it."

"I don't think I can go through with this."

"You don't want to kill him?" I asked, confused. "I thought we wanted him dead."

"That's not what I mean. I still want him gone, but I don't think I can do it like this. Is there another way?"

The change in her tune was surprising. Amber had always been down for the cause, and hearing her want to back out now was frustrating. We'd already gotten through the door. All she had to do was follow through with the plan so we could execute it when I got back.

"I don't think so. After his brother was just killed, I can't see any other way to get close to him. He's going to be on high alert at all times. This is the only way. You just have to work there a few more nights and get him to come home with you. That's all."

"All right," she said with a long sigh. "All right. For Daddy."

"Okay. I need to head out. I should be back sometime tonight. I love you."

"I love you too," she responded, and we disconnected the call.

I stared at the phone momentarily, wondering if I had been insensitive. A part of me wanted to call her back, but I didn't. I didn't plan on returning to the room, so when I got up, I grabbed all my bags before leaving.

Benny owned a packing plant in South Florida, where we had always met. It made it even more convenient to load up my semi. On the way there, I thought deeply about the operation I was forming. I had a few boys, Micah and Ralph, back home, who had been working with Jimmy and me for a while. I felt they would be on board with me. They were loyal and thorough, and I knew they would be willing to put in overtime to get things off the ground. I was sure Amber wouldn't mind helping me to fund her art career for a while.

Before I knew it, I was pulling into the back of Benny's huge warehouse. Upon seeing my vehicle, two workers opened a tall gate and waved me through. I drove to one of the flat-loading areas and parked inside the building. When I did, I saw Benny and a few of his goons standing there, waiting for me. Benny looked like your typical Mafia-type guy: tall, slicked-back hair, always in a suit, and kept a nice timepiece on his wrist. Although I couldn't see their weapons, I knew his goons were strapped with some heat and probably really *were* as menacing as they looked. I grabbed the bag of money I'd brought with me and got out.

Once he laid eyes on me, the rugged look on Benny's face turned to a smile. "Dawg, my old friend," he greeted me smoothly. However, there was something different about him this time. His voice was breathless as if he was using all his energy just to speak. I hadn't noticed it the last time, but he also looked to have gotten skinnier.

"What's good, Benny?"

"You tell me. You're the one who called this meeting."

"Can we go to your office and talk?" I asked, and he nodded.

He and I walked side by side through the busy and loud warehouse. When we got to his office, he made his men stand guard outside the door so we could discuss business privately. I sat across from the gold desk and placed the money bag in the chair beside me.

"Tell me, have you and Jimmy completely sold your last order? If so, that is mighty impressive. You must have some new clientele."

"New clientele is the topic. But no, Jimmy hasn't gotten the last order completely off yet. What he does with it is his business," I said, and Benny raised a brow.

"Don't tell me you're looking to get out of the game when you've barely played yet."

"Nah, I'm actually thinking about stepping it up a notch. That's why I came here." I lifted the money bag off the chair and set it on his desk. "I'm ready to branch off on my own and get some shit going. There's five hundred thousand in that bag. From here on out, I'd like to cop for me and me alone."

"Interesting." Benny leaned forward in his seat and rubbed his chin. "And what about Jimmy? You don't feel that you would be stepping on his toes?"

"I can't step on his toes if he's really moving his feet. His money flow won't stop. I'm just giving myself a new job and a raise. I'll be to him what you are to me. I want what everyone wants . . . to be a king in my own domain. I'm ready to show my face. I'm tired of being a ghost."

"Interesting," he said again.

"Not only that, but I also run the business differently than Jimmy. As I said, I want to be a king, but I never want to get so complacent that I become sloppy."

"Are you saying that Jimmy has become sloppy?"

"I'm saying he ain't Jake. And he ain't me. He'll have to find a new connect if he doesn't tighten up. Best friend or not, I'm not going down for someone else's mistake."

"Smart man. And this operation, you know that if you stay in Atlanta, you'll surely start a war with your friend, right? Money brings out the beast in people, no matter how close you are."

"Jimmy can have Atlanta. My life is done there. I was thinking about—"

"South Florida?" Benny said, interrupting me.

"What?" I asked, confused. "You run South Florida."

"And I am bored," he said with a sigh. "Also, I am sick. Very sick."

"Sick?"

"Cancer." He laughed, although I didn't know what was funny. "You build a life like this for yourself, and then your body turns on you."

"I'm sorry to hear that, Benny."

"Do not be sorry because I'm not. I have lived the life of ten men, but I have only been in love once. And it's my most cherished memory. I hope one day you experience that too."

"What happened?"

"She followed her heart, which led her away from me, but it's okay. I never stopped keeping tabs on her, and I followed her heart too. And in a crazy way, it's led me back to her. But now, I want to go die at home in Cuba. I have been away from my family too long and want to spend my last days with them."

"How far along is your cancer?" I asked.

"Stage four."

"Shit."

"Shit is right. I've been thinking about what I want to do with all *this* shit," he said and quickly waved his hands around. "Of course, my children will take over my legitimate businesses, but what about my other kingdom? They would ruin it and end up in prison faster than I'm dying. They are not built for this life. It is too bloody, too unpredictable. Honestly, you have been on my mind lately, so it's quite a coincidence that you are sitting in front of me today."

"Wait, am I hearing you right? You want *me* to take over your drug empire?"

"Yes. After Jake, I never thought I'd meet another man so much like myself. My kingdom is ready-made. You won't have to worry about stepping on toes. You will have all my clientele, which reaches states over, and some of my most loyal men, if you'll have them. You'll have access to the purest of the pure, and that is power, my boy. So, if you are serious about your inquiry, South Florida is yours for the taking."

"I mean, of course. Passing up an opportunity like this would be foolish, but why not pass the crown to your most loyal? Why me?"

"It's simple. You're not in it simply for the money. You come from money. You're in it for the love of the game, which means you have the true heart of a hustler. I have never been one to think that a torch passes to the next simply by birthright or favor. It should go to the most qualified. In my eyes, that's you."

I almost wanted to pinch myself to see if I was still dreaming. Regardless of how good of a businessman I was, things like that didn't happen every day. I wasn't naïve. I knew it wouldn't be easy taking over what someone else built, and there would be people who opposed me as head of the operation. However, if and when they did, they would meet the dog in me.

I nodded. "I'm with it. I have some things to wrap up back home," I told him, and he took the money from the desk.

"I will have your order ready when you get back."

"Cool," I said and stood up to leave. Before I was out the door, I looked back at him. "Do me a favor, and don't die before I make it back."

Chapter Twenty-two

Theo

"Fuck," I moaned with my head back.
I was standing in the middle of my office, holding a handful of blond hair as I guided a skillful mouth up and down my shaft. I rammed my tip into the back of her throat simply because the choking sound made my meat even harder. I looked down and watched Bunny go to work, sucking and slurping like her job depended on it—because it did. As she sucked, I slapped the side of her face and began thrusting faster into her mouth. I didn't care if she could keep up. I didn't even care if she could breathe. I felt my nut nearing its escape window, and when I was ready to explode, I pulled out and ejaculated on her face.
"Shit," I said, jacking the rest of my semen out.
When I finished, I stumbled backward and fell into my desk chair. I caught my breath with my eyes closed, and when I opened them, I saw Bunny wiping off her face with some tissues I kept on my desk. Something about getting mine made me instantly disgusted with whoever had helped me get it.
In truth, I had been disgusted with her last night when I had to settle for her instead of Star. However, when I went to look for Star, I saw her and Myleek exiting his office. So, instead, I had to settle for the snow bunny. Her

pussy and head were good, but it wasn't what I wanted. And I hated not getting what I wanted.

She tried to sit on my lap, but I pushed her off. "You can leave," I said, and she looked confused.

"Did I do something wrong?"

"Nah, but you served your purpose," I said, grabbing some hundreds from my desk. I threw them in her direction. "Get dressed and get out. And you better be here on time for work tonight."

She didn't say another word, but I could tell her feelings were hurt. She'd have to get a thicker skin if she planned on working at Razberry, especially since that wasn't the last time I planned on using her to satisfy me. The moment anybody stepped into my club, I owned them. That was why I didn't know what the hell Myleek was thinking touching Star first.

I went into the bathroom connected to my office and showered before getting dressed. Then I left my office and went down the hallway to see if my brother was still there. His office was empty. I couldn't wait until Star came into work tonight. I had something in store for her.

I walked down the hallway and stopped in front of Dell's office. The sadness I felt from losing him had faded, and I didn't know if it was because there was really a monster inside of me that wouldn't allow me to let any feeling but anger linger. Although his death was a direct consequence of what we had done, it was meant to send me a message. Clearly, Jimmy wasn't afraid of me. My thirst for revenge had nothing to do with Dell being dead because *I* was still alive. No, it was about my respect. And because of that, Jimmy had to die.

Almost right on cue, I felt my phone vibrate in my pocket, and when I pulled it out, I saw a rat emoji on my screen.

"What's the word?" I said when I answered.

"He on the move. I'd give him 'bout an hour before he hits the stroll."

"Yup," I said, knowing what that meant, and hung up.

Just like Jake hadn't known, Jimmy didn't know a rat was in his camp. The rat's name was John John, and all it took was a little extra pocket change every month for him to keep me hip to Jimmy's business. I knew more than anyone thought I did, like the fact that Jimmy had a silent partner who helped him move how he moved—some ghost who went by the name of Dawg. I always wondered how he moved his weight so efficiently. I'd done my digging but couldn't come up with anything. In due time, I'd figure it out.

Stepping away from Dell's office door, I went to the girls' dressing room. It was only around eleven, and I knew most of the girls weren't there that early, but I could always count on Vicious to be present. Most times, because she got so drunk and high, she couldn't drive home from work. And just like I thought, there she was, passed out on the pink velour couch I'd put in there for them.

"Wake up," I said and patted her cheek.

"Mmm." She stirred and then leaned up and stretched. "It's time for work again already? I feel like I just went to sleep."

"No, but I need you to go on a side quest," I said.

"What's in it for me?" she asked.

"A big stack of money," I told her, and she smiled.

"You know I like money. What you need me to do?"

"I need you to go somewhere with Myleek today," I said, and her smile got even bigger. "I need you to go to the stroll."

"The stroll? Nigga, I ain't no prostitute."

"Don't act like you ain't never fucked for no bread before, Vicious. You the last one to be acting like a saint. Plus, you ain't even gotta fuck him. I just need you to keep him busy enough so Leek can get to him."

"So, a setup? A'ight, I'm down. I need some bands for this, though. More than the last time," she said.

It wasn't the first time I'd used Vicious as bait. Usually, it was just when someone ran off with my money, and I used her to track them down. She did her job well, and out of all the bitches here, she was the only one I trusted. Well, as much as I *could* trust another person, but even she was disposable.

"I got you. Now, get up and wash your ass. I need you ready as soon as possible," I told her, and before I walked away, I looked at her. "And no funny business with my brother. He's moved on anyway. He was fucking Star in his office last night."

"What?" Her eyes grew wide with surprise and hurt. "That new bitch you stopped me from crashing last night?"

"I won't stop you tonight," I threw over my shoulder.

I left her to get ready and smirked, realizing I was killing two birds with one stone. Vicious was crazy about Leek and did everything she could to keep the other girls away from him. Finding out that one slipped through the cracks wouldn't sit well with her, and a good beat down was the perfect punishment for Star.

I hurried back up to the office hallway and knocked on Leek's door. I hoped he was there and hadn't gone home, but when I heard movement on the other side of the door, I knew he hadn't left.

"Yo," he said sleepily when he opened the door, shirtless.

"What got you so tired? You never sleep in this late." I glanced behind him and saw that he was inside by himself.

"I had a good-ass night, that's all."

"I bet you did. I thought I told you I don't like you sampling the merchandise before me," I said, unable to contain the sudden anger that flared inside me. "You knew I wanted Star. You stepped on my toes."

"I ain't step on shit. I been knew shorty before she stepped up in here. And she ain't no merchandise. Last night was her first and last day."

"We'll see." I chuckled. "These bitches is all the same, little brother. Just after a trick who needs a nut. You'll see. Anyway, I got some work for you."

"Right now? I'm sleepy."

"I know where Jimmy gon' be at in the next hour. And he gon' be by himself," I told him and watched him wake all the way up.

"Where?" he asked quickly.

"That nigga got a taste for them dirty hoes on the stroll over there by the old Windmoor projects. I got word that he's headed there soon, and I need you to take Vicious—"

"Hell nah. I'll go clap that nigga by myself."

"No, she's going with you. She's the perfect bait. Get ready. Meet me downstairs in five minutes," I said, and he shut his door.

I returned to my office to grab the keys to an old, unmarked Hyundai Sonata with tinted windows parked outside Razberry. It was one of many throwaway cars I had for times like this. When I got down to the main floor, Leek and Vicious were already there waiting for me. Her lace outfit and jean jacket would make her blend in well with the girls on the stroll. I handed Leek the keys and dapped him up.

"Handle that for me," I said when I pulled him in for a quick embrace.

"You mean for Dell," he said, and I grinned sheepishly.

"Yeah, for him too," I said.

He turned and walked out of Razberry with Vicious following him like a lost puppy. I expected the next phone call from him to tell me Jimmy was dead.

I didn't know how I ended up at our family home, where we'd all grown up. It was an older Victorian-style home that my parents had remodeled many times until Mama was happy with it. I realized as I walked up the steps that led to the front door that she was the reason I was there. It was apparent that I was nowhere near her favorite son, and I felt it was time for us to talk. I couldn't shake the things she'd said to me at Dell's funeral and then how she embarrassed me at my trial.

When I got to the door, I used my key to unlock it, but to my surprise, it wouldn't even turn. When had she changed the locks? I tried my other key, but it was the same thing. I was forced to ring the doorbell and wait for someone to open it. Clara, Mama's housekeeper, who was even older than her, opened the door. She didn't look too pleased to see me.

"Theo, what are you doing here?"

"I came to see Mama. Is she home?"

"Yes, but she wasn't expecting company this morning," Clara told me. "Maybe you should come back later."

"Nah, I'm here now. Can I come into my own house?" I asked, and she hesitated before forcing a smile to her face.

"Of course, come in," she said, moving out of the way as I stepped inside. "I'll go tell her you're here. Wait in the kitchen."

"I'll be in the living room," I said, heading in that direction. I didn't like her telling me what to do like I was still a child. She worked for my family, *not* the other way around. Clara had been with us since I was a kid, and I wasn't her favorite person, either. It might have had something to do with all the pranks I'd played on her. My favorite was putting itching powder in her wig right before she went to church. I smirked, thinking about how mad she was when she came home. Mama and Dad gave her a week off fully paid because of that.

I looked around the house, and everything seemed to be how I remembered it. Mama always had an eye for design, and the living room had an old England royal feel. There was even a cushioned throne chair that my dad used to sit in and read the paper. I plopped down in it as I continued to scan the room.

My eyes fell on the family wall where Mama had our photos lined on the wall and ledges. The more I looked, the more it felt like someone had their hand around my heart and was squeezing it. I saw photos of my parents and my brothers, but every picture of me had been taken down or replaced. I jumped back up to get a closer look to make sure I wasn't tripping. I wasn't. There were *no* photos of me on the family wall.

"What are you doing here, Theo?" Mama's voice sounded behind me.

I turned around and saw her fully dressed in a comfortable two-piece suit. She didn't even try to hide the annoyance in her voice or face. I stared at her like it was my first time ever seeing her. "I came to ask you something."

"Well, ask, so you can go run the streets or hang out at your titty bar, or whatever it is you like to do because it sure isn't run the family businesses. Leek does that, right?"

"*I* run all this shit. Me. Nothing would go round without me."

"Yeah," she chortled. "Keep telling yourself that."

"When you take my pictures down?" I asked. "After Dell died?"

"I took those down way before that. But you wouldn't have known since you're so self-centered and invested," she said coldly.

"Why?"

"Because frankly, although I birthed you and raised you as best as I could, I don't like you very much, Theo. And I don't like seeing your face. I don't understand how something that can look so much like me be so fucked up."

"Why do you hate me, Mama?" I asked, feeling a lump form in my throat.

There weren't many people in the world who could hurt my feelings. Truthfully, I didn't think she was one of them. But every word that came out of her mouth felt like a dagger to my chest. I didn't know what I had done to be so targeted by her mean side.

"You know what?" she said and touched her chin. "I never thought about it like that. *Do* I hate you? I hate the way that you *think* you're the head of this family, but you do nothing for anyone but yourself. I hate the embarrassment you bring to this family because of your stupid ego, which leads you to make stupid decisions."

"I don't make stupid decisions."

"Ha. You know I'm the one who had to clean up the situation with that girl you killed in that motel room. She called me that night, crying and begging me to save her. I tried to get there, but you had already slit her throat and rode off into the sunset. You're lucky that I got there when I did and talked that poor homeless bastard into going in there and robbing her. He was still in there rummaging through her purse when the police arrived. Now, he's in jail for a murder *you* committed. And that shit is on my soul because of you."

She was talking about Reesie, one of Razberry's old girls. She'd gotten too clingy, and I didn't trust that if I let her go, she wouldn't run to the police about my illegal dealings. So, I had to get rid of her permanently. I didn't know Mama knew about that.

"Mama, that wasn't my fault."

"It was. You prey on those girls, and it makes me sick that you're so perverted. Business is one thing, but thinking you're a god who can do whatever you want whenever you want is another. It makes me sick that your father and I could make something as heinous as you. I can't remember the last time you even made me crack a smile. You *disgust* me."

"I'm the head of this family!" I shouted.

"You sound like a kid throwing a tantrum. Theodore Elliott Lavy, you aren't the head of a damn thing but your own bullshit. You are a disgrace to your father's name, and it's your fault my son is dead. You've always had this hold over my babies, and I always knew you'd be the reason they get hurt. And I was right." She clutched her chest as tears started to fall from her eyes. "You are poison. And I don't want you here or in my life. You got my baby killed. Cordell is dead because of you, and you know what? I wish it were you instead of him in that casket."

I didn't know what came over me, but her words caused a chain reaction in my mind, heart, and physical body. I didn't even realize I had swung until I saw her face snap back and her nose break. But I didn't stop there. I continued to punch her anywhere my fists would land. Because you know what? I hated her too. I hated how she always put me down. I hated how she spoke to me. I hated how she didn't support me. And I hated how she didn't love me like she loved my brothers. If I couldn't have her love as a mother, nobody could. I beat her until there was barely any life in her left, and it felt *good*.

I laughed when I stood up and saw her twitching because she couldn't move. I laughed so hard at her dying body as I caught my breath. I could have finished her there, but I wanted her to suffer the same way she wanted me to suffer at her tongue-lashings.

"Fuck you," I said and spat on her.

"Oh my God!"

I heard the sound of glass shattering and looked up to see Clara walking in on the murderous scene. She had a pitcher of sweet tea in her hands and dropped it at the sight of Mama on the ground. She froze for a second with a look of terror before her hand shakily made its way to her mouth, and she shook her head.

"When you were a little boy, I told them you were evil. I saw it in your eyes. You're the devil, boy. The devil."

"Nah, I'm Theo," I said right before rushing her and wrapping my hands around her throat.

Chapter Twenty-three

Myleek

I drove in silence in the direction of where my brother told me Jimmy was going to be. The closer I got, the more my trigger finger itched. I wanted to put him down, and I wanted him down *badly*. Bad enough to even work with Vicious to do it. She was surprisingly quiet as she sat in the passenger seat, but her face read like she had an attitude.

"Is it true?" she finally asked, and I ignored her because I didn't know what she was talking about. "Myleek, is it true?"

"Is what true?" I snapped.

"You fucked that bitch Star last night?" she asked and actually had hurt in her voice. "Theo told me."

I sighed, annoyed because I didn't know why Theo would tell her something like that. It wasn't her business. For the life of me, I also couldn't understand why the girl was so pressed about what *I* did. I'd told her many times that I didn't want her. One, she fucked my brother when she first started. Two, she just wasn't what I saw myself with in the future. When I thought about the usual things like settling down and having a family, she wasn't the one I could see raising my children. She'd sold herself a dream and not only bought it, but she also believed it. I also knew how she tried to run off anybody interested in me. But she wouldn't do that to Amber because I *wanted* Amber. And there was *nothing* Vicious could do about it.

"I did. I loved it. Probably gon' do it a lot," I said evenly, knowing my words were landing on her like bricks.

"Why would you do that to me? I thought eventually we would be together."

"The fuck do you mean? You delusional or something? How often do I have to tell you that *nothing* is going on between us? We fucked, I needed a nut, and you got some bread for it. That was the exchange. I never promised you my heart, and I never will."

"So, what's so different about her?" she asked jealously.

"She's *her*," I said simply.

Finally, we arrived at the stroll, just a long sidewalk popular for working girls to be at. I could already see small groups of women spread out along the street. Some were walking and pandering to traffic. Others were smoking or taking pictures of themselves. I saw a few get picked up and hoped we hadn't missed our mark.

"A'ight, we here. Get out and work the stroll. If anybody asks who you are, tell 'em to get out your face and that your daddy is in a car watching you. Understand? I'm finna send you a picture of the target now. Only get in the car for him."

"Duh, that's why we're here. You better be watching me so a motherfucka doesn't kill me."

I sent her the photo of Jimmy that I had on my phone. She looked at it and nodded, understanding. I let her out a little ways away and let her walk the rest of the way to the stroll. She never left my sight. I hoped Jimmy would show soon because as soon as Vicious started walking, cars started slowing down on her. She kept waving them away because they weren't Jimmy.

I watched her every move for what felt like forever, until a silver G-Wagon hit the corner and slowed up on her. I leaned up when I noticed her interacting differently with him. She smiled big and got in the car with him. I could only assume she was with Jimmy, and the second they pulled off, I began following a few cars behind them.

They turned off into an alley, and I parked by a dumpster. I opened the glove compartment in the car, and sure enough, Theo had a ski mask inside it. I put it on and grabbed my pistol from under my seat. I checked the magazine to make sure it was full because I wanted to open Jimmy's body up like cheese. I waited a few minutes before getting out so Vicious had enough time to start doing her thing before I ran up on them. I didn't think my heart would be pounding so hard, but the thought of getting my get-back for my brother had my adrenaline going crazy.

Finally, I got out of the car and gently shut the door before crouching and hitting the alley's corner. The G-Wagon was parked halfway down it. I crept up on the passenger side so he wouldn't see me in his rearview. The G-Wagon wasn't moving at all, and that should have been the first red flag. But when I upped my pistol to shoot into the car, I was surprised to see Jimmy with his pistol pointed at me. I jumped out of the way the moment he started shooting. Instead of pulling off, I heard his door open and shut, letting me know he was ready to get in the field with me.

"You musta pissed that bitch off," Jimmy shouted as he stalked me around the Benz. "As soon as she got in the whip, she sang like a bird about y'all setup. She was a bad bitch too. I hate that I had to put a bullet in her head. That body is on you, though, Myleek."

The fact that he said my name let me know that Vicious really had snitched. She was that mad at me for being involved with Amber that she would turn on the people that fed her. I prayed to God Amber and I could work out because I didn't want to deal with another delusional woman in my life. Hell, I hoped *I* made it out of this shoot-out so I could see her again.

"Fuck that bitch. I don't care about her being dead," I said and kept crouching as I moved around the car.

I didn't want to give him an open shot. I glanced through the window at the passenger-side rearview mirror and saw that he was toward the back door on the other side. With no hesitation, I stood up and got to blowing. He had no choice but to fall back, and I took that opportunity to run him down. However, he was a crafty dude. While I was running around the Benz, he dove under it and shimmied back to the driver's seat. He put the car in drive and sped away with his door still open. That didn't stop me from trying to air him down, though. I shot my gun until it clicked. When he was toward the end of the alley, he stopped and pushed Vicious's body out of the car and kept on going. I knew I needed to get scarce too.

I ran back to the car, hopped in, and sped off. My heart was racing at the near-death situation, but I was more mad at myself for being that close to Jimmy and not being able to take him down.

"Fuck," I shouted and hit the steering wheel as I drove.

I tried calling Theo, but his phone went straight to voicemail. My mind was all over the place. Now, Jimmy knew we were after him, and we would need to watch our backs like crazy. I hated moving around with too many shooters. It attracted too much attention, but that might've been what needed to be done.

I drove the car to the demolition site my father bought when we were kids that we now owned. I marked the car for destruction before getting into another unmarked throwaway Theo had parked at the site. That one was an ugly blue Saturn, but I didn't care. I snatched my mask from my face and debated returning to Razberry. In the end, I realized I needed to be around some love. All Theo was going to do was tell me how badly I'd fucked up anyway, and I was already mad at myself. I didn't need to hear that right then.

I drove to my mama's house, hoping she could offer me some consolation. When I arrived, I parked and knew she would ask me whose ugly car I was driving. I took a breath and got out to go inside. Once at the door, I pulled out my key and unlocked it. As soon as I walked in, something felt different. A trail of broken glass and liquid was by the front door. I stepped inside, and all at once, I almost stumbled back out.

"What . . . the fuck?" I said out loud as I stood in the foyer, looking at the stairs.

Lying dead was our caretaker, Clara. I knew she was dead by the way her eyes were frozen open, looking at the ceiling. She wasn't moving or breathing, but still, I went to her and checked her pulse. Her body was still warm, but she was gone. She had bruising on her neck as if she'd been strangled to death. My thoughts instantly went to my mother.

"Mama?" I called.

I pulled out my gun to search the rest of the house, only to remember I'd used all the bullets. If someone were still inside, I'd have to take them out with my bare hands. I first crept into the kitchen, but nobody was there. The next place I went was the living room, and the visual there made me drop to my knees. Blood splatters were everywhere, and lying on the ground, bludgeoned, was Mama. I crawled to her and scooped her up in my arms. The moment I did, she gave a little choked gasp. She was alive but barely clinging on.

"Leek," she whispered.

"Mama, who did this?"

"Leek, be careful. He's . . . evil."

"Who, Mama? Who did this?"

"T-Theo."

"Theo? No. He wouldn't."

"He's . . . evil. Check . . . cameras."

"Mama, please don't leave me. Please don't leave me!"

"I . . . love you, Myleek. My . . . baby boy. I want to see your father and Dell now."

She'd exhausted all her energy. I wondered if she held on just long enough in hopes someone would come so she could tell who did it to her. I felt her body grow stiff in my arms and knew she was gone. But even still, I was in denial.

"Mama," I cried. "Mama!"

I clutched her body so tightly to mine as if I were trying to will some of my life force to enter her. My run-in with Jimmy was pushed to the furthest part of my mind as my head dropped to her knotted forehead. I sobbed with my whole chest, allowing my tears to mix with her blood.

Chapter Twenty-four

Jimmy

I drove like my life depended on it—because it did. I didn't know if Myleek Lavy was still after me. The last thing I expected to happen that day was to get into a shoot-out or be targeted. I couldn't remember the last time I'd been caught lacking, and if it weren't for that ho being in her feelings, I'd be a dead man. Not much shook me, but I was definitely shaken. My mind went a thousand miles a minute as I tried to figure out how it happened. I could have been set up, or maybe they'd been watching me since I killed their brother. Either way, I should have been ready for them to come. I'd been moving recklessly. But that stopped immediately.

I looked down and noticed my arm was bleeding. My adrenaline was pumping so hard I didn't feel pain anywhere. Still, I checked myself to make sure I hadn't been hit. I didn't see any actual bullet wounds, but I did see where a chunk of flesh on my right forearm was missing from where I must have been grazed. The windows in my G-Wagon were completely gone, and blood was in the passenger seat from where I'd killed the girl. I had to hop whips quickly.

I drove to my garage and stashed the Benz until I could figure out what to do with it. Next, I hopped into the Honda Civic I'd gotten after I killed Cordell.

I sped to the trap, checking my rearview in a paranoid manner. The last thing I needed was to get pulled over by them people wearing blood-soaked clothes. When I got there, I burst through the doors. Mula, John John, and my boy DeJuan were bagging up powder to run, but they instantly stopped when they saw me. Mula jumped up in concern, while John John looked surprised as ever to see me.

"Yo, cuz, what the fuck happened to you?" Mula asked me with wide eyes.

"Myleek Lavy tried to run down on me," I said and showed my arm. "Go get me some alcohol and a wrap."

DeJuan hopped up and ran to grab the first aid kit. Mula clutched at his gun angrily. I could see him getting madder and madder the longer he looked at me.

"Where were you at when this happened?" he asked.

"It don't even matter. He did it."

"It do matter. 'Cause that mean that motherfucka been watching you."

"He probably was over there with them bitches on the stroll," John John commented, and I whipped my head to him.

"What makes you say that?" I asked and saw a nervous look overcome him.

"Shit." He shrugged. "You always over there. Anybody coulda clocked that. Easy setup."

He was right, but still, something about his demeanor was throwing me off. Maybe it was because my nerves were still bad from being shot at. But I was taught at an early age to trust my gut.

DeJuan returned with the first aid kit, and Mula assisted me with my wound. "This shit gon' hurt, cuz," he warned before pouring alcohol over my wound.

"Fuck," I shouted in pain as the sting overtook my entire body.

"I told you," he said, putting some gauze over the wound before wrapping it.

"You done did this shit too many times."

"Shit, I done got shot too many times. I'm a pro now. And, cuz, you need to leave them hoes alone. For real, them bitches is scandalous."

"I ain't gon' have no choice. It's gon' be us or them at this point. And I'm banking on us."

"You know I'm with you 'til the end," Mula said.

"I gotta get rid of the G-Wagon. It's fucked up and stained. And I left a body."

"Where?" John John chimed in.

I looked at him and saw the eagerness on his face. Once again, the hairs on the back of my neck stood up. Not because he was asking questions, but because he was asking the *wrong* questions. He hadn't even been worried about my health. If it were the other way around, I would make sure the boss was straight, especially if that was the hand that fed me. My instinct was faster than my thoughts.

I pulled my gun out and aimed it at his face. "Let me see ya phone, nigga," I said.

"What? You trippin'," John John said nervously and looked at Mula. "Mu, tell this nigga he tripping."

"What you on, cuz?" Mula asked me.

"Something just off with this motherfucka, man. You just spoke on the direct setup when I ain't even say nothing. Now you asking about where bodies is at. That's weird. I need that phone. Now!"

"Let him see ya phone," Mula said and upped his pole on John John too.

John John looked back and forth between the guns on him. He sighed and went into his pocket to get his phone. The moment he was about to hand it to me, he hit my gun out of my hand and tried to book it out the front door. Mula was too quick for him. He hit him with the butt of his gun so hard in the temple that it dropped him instantly.

"You shoulda shot that motherfucka."

"Nigga, this a .40. Shit woulda been too loud. Get his phone. If he on flaw shit, we gon' wrap this motherfucka up and take him to the woods."

I picked up my gun and went into John John's pockets to find his phone. When my hand wrapped around it, I pulled it out and used his finger to unlock it. It didn't take long to realize that I had a snake around me for way too long. I sat down and scrolled through it. I saw many phone calls and texts between him and Theo, dating back to when Jake was killed. The only thing he hadn't told Theo was where the new trap was, and I was sure that was because when Theo killed Jake, he left no survivors. John John was always in the trap, doing something. He must not have wanted to risk his life.

The rage in me was like fire. I was so mad that I was numb. I looked at the man lying knocked out in front of me and simply nodded my head. "Put some tarp down in the back and tie him up. Cover his mouth real good. I want you two to chop off every piece of his body while he's still alive. Start with his dick and end up with his head."

My voice was even and smooth, but there was an icy undertone when I gave the order. Mula and DeJuan nodded as they dragged him to the back room. I leaned back on the couch and looked up at the ceiling. Just another day in the office.

A knock at the door caught my attention. I clutched my gun as I got up and crept to the door. When I peeked through the peephole, I was relieved to see that it was only Dawg. I opened the door, and his eyes instantly went to the blood all over my shirt.

"The fuck happened to you now, Jimmy?" he asked in a fed-up tone when he stepped in.

"That nigga Myleek Lavy. He tried to get me," I said, thinking he would be as ready to go as Mula, but to my surprise, he had no sympathy.

"What you think would happen? You killed his brother."

"Because they killed mine," I said and instantly stopped talking when he gave me a knowing look.

"I knew you were lying the first time I asked. You said you didn't do it. Now, you want to be honest. You're hot as fuck, Jimmy." He shook his head at me.

"No, *we're* hot as fuck. We at war!"

"This is a war I'm not involving myself in. You're going to get yourself killed. I have things I want to live for."

"They killed my brother," I repeated.

"And you killed theirs. You're even."

"We won't be even until they're all dead."

"Then that's something you'll do alone," he said.

"Jake is the one who put you on, and you're acting like you don't give a fuck."

"No, I'm the *only* one who gives a fuck. Jake didn't move as carelessly and stupidly as you. Killing motherfuckas in public, having drugs and guns in the same spot all the time, getting shot at and shit . . . That's not the life of a boss. You're moving like a runner. A little nigga."

"A runner? Little nigga?" I scoffed and took a step back to rub my chin. "You know what? I shoulda known you'd start acting funny because of this whole Benny shit. News flash, nigga. You can't cop from him without me. Without *my* money. The connect came from me. And maybe you don't need to be down with me anymore since that's how you're moving."

"Nah, it came from Jake. And Jake ain't here no more," he said and sighed. "I didn't come here to argue with you. But I'm glad we're on the same page regarding that. I'm out."

"What you mean you're out?"

"You can run all of this by yourself. I had a meeting with Benny yesterday—"

"So, now, you doing shit behind my back?"

"*All* you do is shit behind *my* back. I had to do what's best for me. And what's best for me is to branch out independently."

"So you're taking my connect?"

"No, I *am* your new connect. I'm moving to Florida and taking over Benny's operation. He gave me his blessing. And I'm leaving here as soon as I wrap up some business," he said, and I could tell he was serious. "You can keep everything we just copped so you'll be able to re-up alone next time, but I'm telling you, Jimmy, if you don't tighten up, I can't do business with you."

"You can't do business with *me?*" I said with a laugh. Nothing was funny. I was just in disbelief.

"You heard me. I came here out of respect for my brother."

"Nah, you ain't got no brother no more. You the boss now, remember? Get the fuck outta my shit. Now," I barked.

He stared at me for a moment and shook his head. Then he pointed at my injury.

"Take care of that. When you cool down, hit me up," he said and left the way he'd come in.

As he left, too many emotions were going through my body. I was angry, and I felt betrayed. I stood there staring at the door as my hands slowly balled into fists so tight I could feel my nails digging through my skin. Allun Halloway, the schoolboy? The lawyer? The square that I raised up into a soldier becoming the plug? Was not gonna happen. That was *my* position. Little did he know, he wouldn't make it to Florida, or at least not with his heart. I planned to do to him the same thing I did to the last motherfucka who tried to ruin my life.

Chapter Twenty-five

Amber

I slow danced around my room, thinking about my night with Leek. Even if I tried not to think about him, my body wouldn't let me. One, my kitty was still sore from the pounding I'd received, and two, I could still feel his cum sliding out of my rear most of the day. Some might have thought it was nasty, but to me, it was art. And it was romantic to have a remnant of him inside of me. I believed in love at first sight, but I never thought it would happen to me.

Leek had given me my first dose of happiness since the death of my father, and for that, I would always be grateful. Although I told Dawg I'd do what needed to be done, I wanted to find another way to get Theo myself in a way that Leek would never know I was involved. He didn't have anything to do with my father's death, and I didn't want *him* involved at all. However, I knew killing his brother might break his heart, which was why I needed to be a ghost about it.

I did plan on going to the club that night, not to work but to get the money I'd left in Leek's office. It was mine, and I'd earned it. Plus, I just wanted a reason to see him in private. We didn't have to have sex again, but some more kisses would be nice. I didn't realize how much I'd yearned for affection until he held me in his arms.

I was still humming to the slow jams playing in my room and moving my body when someone knocked at the door. I turned around when the door opened and saw Lina standing there with her arms folded, smirking at me. The twinkle in her eye forced a grin on my face.

"What?" I asked.

"So, where were you at so late last night?" she asked.

"Not you in my business," I said, laughing.

"I stay in your business," she said, inviting herself to sit on my bed. She patted the spot next to her. "Now, come on. Spill the tea or whatever you young girls say these days."

"If I tell you, you can't tell Dawg," I said and held up my pinky finger when I sat down.

"I promise," she said, linking her pinky with mine. "Now, tell me. Who is he? Is he handsome?"

"Lina, he's *fine,* and I *really* like him. He even came to my art show," I told her, and her eyes lit up. "He just makes me feel like a woman. And last night, he *really* made me feel like a woman."

"Oh, mi amor . . . I love this for you," Lina said, cupping my cheek with her hand. "You deserve this and so much more. Why don't you want Dawg to know? He would be happy that you're happy."

"Because this guy, he's the brother of Dawg's enemy. Of my enemy. It's like a forbidden love, Lina. But I can't let it go. I think it's the real thing."

As I spoke, I felt tears come to my eyes and saw understanding come to hers. She didn't judge me. In fact, she didn't say a word. Instead, she hugged me so tightly that she didn't *need* to say a word. When she pulled away, she kissed me on my forehead and placed her hand on my heart.

"This will tell you which way to go. Dawg will always love you. You don't have to follow that trail. It will always be there. But that one might need to be explored just a little more before you decide. Dawg lives a dangerous life and will make many enemies along the way. Unfortunately, some of those enemies might not be bad people. They're just on the wrong side of things."

"Why are you so wise? And why doesn't any of this scare you?" I asked her, and she gave a faraway smile.

"A while ago, I dated a man. Cuban guy, real sweet and handsome. He was in the life, and I saw many, many things. I saw him kill people. I saw him save people. And I saw him make a hell of a lot of money. He wanted me to ride off into the sunset with him. And I would have, but then your mom died, and you kids needed me more. I followed my heart then, and it led me straight to you and Dawg. Something told me there would be a day when you needed me more than ever, and I was right. I have no regrets, and I hope he's happy wherever he is."

"I love you," I said, and it was my turn to hug her tightly as she rubbed my back.

"And I love you more," she said. "But now, I need you to come downstairs. There's someone here to see you."

"Who?"

"Come see," she said, then pointed at the shorts and cami I wore. "But put some clothes on first. I don't care how old you get. Look presentable for company."

I laughed and got up to find some clothes in my closet. When she left, I hopped in the shower for a fast minute to wash the last of Myleek off me and hurried to throw on a pair of leggings and a T-shirt. Before leaving my room, I slid on a pair of fuzzy house slippers and bound down the stairs. When I got there, I was pleasantly surprised to see Jeffrey standing in the living room, waiting for me.

"Jeffrey," I said and hugged him tightly.

"Hey, Tink," he said, kissing my cheek before pulling away. "I just wanted to come check on you. I'm sorry I haven't reached out much since the funeral."

"I understand. This whole situation is triggering. But I'm glad you stopped by."

"How's everything? With the art and all that?"

"My piece sold for a hundred thousand dollars at the art showcase. Antonio emailed me around Daddy's funeral and wants me to submit another for his Paris showcase, but I don't know."

"A hundred thousand dollars? Girl, you better follow that dream. Shiiiit, don't play with yourself now. It's okay to be sad, but go cry in Paris, baby," Jeffrey said, and I laughed.

"You're right. We'll see."

"Uh-huh. How's Dawg? I see he hasn't been to the office. I'm assuming he's done?"

"I think that's a safe thing to say."

"Good for him. He was a great lawyer, but even a blind person could see that wasn't where his heart was. I hope he finds something that makes him happy."

"We haven't decided what we will do with the firm yet. I don't want to end my father's legacy, but—"

"It's over, honey," Jeffrey said. "He lived a good life."

"But what will you do?"

"Baby, I'm retiring. Your father set me up nicely in his will. Hell, I might start me up a little business or two."

"I'm so happy for you. At least some good came out of all this bad," I said.

"I'ma miss him, though. I'ma miss him a lot," Jeffrey said, wiping the corners of his eyes. "But let me get out of here before we're swimming in a pool of tears. I just wanted to see how you were doing. You know I'm just a phone call away."

"I know. I love you," I said and gave him another embrace.

"And I love you too," he said, and when we pulled away, he made his way to the front door. But before he hit the hallway, he turned to face me. "And, honey?"

"Yeah?"

"Whoever got you walking funny, keep him, okay?" He winked at me, and then he was gone.

That evening couldn't come fast enough. I didn't know how I would evade Theo at the club that night, but I was going to try. I was one and done, and he could do nothing about it. I drove my Range Rover to Razberry and parked in the employee parking lot. It was a little early, so there weren't too many cars there. I was still on cloud nine as I prepared to get out of my vehicle. But before I could open the door, my phone rang, and I looked down at my brother's face.

"Hello?" I answered.

"You at the club?" he asked.

"Yeah, you looking at my location?" I said, getting out of my car and walking toward the building.

"I always check your location. I think tonight should be the night."

"Dawg, I really think we should figure out another way," I said into the phone.

"I told you there's no other way."

I hadn't even taken five steps away from my car when I heard quick footsteps approaching me. I turned around to see who it was, and my eyes widened when I saw a masked figure coming at me fast with something metal in their hands.

"What the fuck are you doing?" I screamed as they tried to grab me. "Get off me!"

"What's going on?" Dawg's voice came through the phone.

"Dawg, help me!" I screamed as the masked figure tugged me and made me drop the phone. "Stop!"

I took a deep breath to scream as loud as I could, but before a sound came out, I was hit with a hard object across the head, forcing me to fall to the ground. Everything went dark on the way down.

Chapter Twenty-six

Myleek

I'd seen a lot of things, but the worst sight I ever saw was my own brother beating our mother to death. I did as Mama said and played the cameras back. Sure enough, it was Theo who was responsible for her death and Clara's. It was hard to watch because it wasn't an accident. It was intentional. He didn't hold back one ounce of strength when he was hitting or choking the women. I knew my brother was heartless and a killer, but I didn't know he had it in him to turn on his own family. If he could kill our mother, the woman who birthed him, what would he do to me? I thought something was off about how quickly he moved on after Dell's death, and even how he made it about himself, but I thought that maybe it was just how he'd chosen to mourn. But no, we were *all* just disposable to him. It was his world, and we were just living in it.

I couldn't even say I was caught between a rock and a hard place. There was only one thing that had to happen. He had to go. I couldn't trust him. Anyone who rejected or opposed him met their demise, and I'd done something he didn't like. I took something he wanted—something that I also wasn't letting go of. There was no telling how he would punish me for that, and I wouldn't risk it. Fury coursed through my body after watching him take my mama from me. He was everything she said he was—and worse.

I erased the camera footage in the house, not to protect him but because prison would be too kind for him. Theo was the kind of man who would go to prison and run the place. It wouldn't be punishment. It would be just another kingdom. I wanted him to feel the exact pain he gave my mama.

I waited for the coroners to get there, and that took longer than I expected, and then I had to give the pigs a statement. But after that, I was a speed racer all the way to Razberry. I knew he would be there. He was a sociopath in his dominion.

When I arrived, I saw his car parked in the front, so I pulled in the back. That way, I could take the stairs directly up to our offices. Once inside, I took the stairs by two, and when I got to his office, I opened the door without knocking. I was sickened to see him sitting at his desk with one of the new girls, Bunny. He was sucking her nipples and playing with her pussy like those hands hadn't just committed the ultimate crime.

"What the fuck, Leek? I'm busy," he said dismissively. But then he suddenly popped his head around Bunny to look at me. "Hey, did you handle that earlier?"

"That's what I'm here to talk to you about," I said, looking at Bunny. "Get the fuck out."

She looked at Theo, and he waved her away. She pulled the top of her dress back up and hopped down from the desk. When she walked past me, she rolled her eyes at me, and I couldn't help but grab her by the back of her head and launch her out of the room to get her gone faster. I heard a thud as she hit the wall outside the office, but I didn't care. I was tired of his hoes. I was tired of *him*.

I shut the door behind me and focused on Theo, who had gotten up from his seat and come around his desk. He leaned on it and shrugged his shoulders at me.

"So, is the nigga dead?" he asked.

"Nah, he ain't fuckin' dead. That bitch Vicious is, though," I told him, and he let out an angry sigh.

"How the fuck you let her get killed?"

"Because your stupid ass told her I fucked Star, and she got mad as fuck. When she got in Jimmy's car, she told him it was a setup, and that nigga started blowing at me the second I got to the whip."

"Damn," Theo said, and then started laughing. "I only told her that so she would beat Star's ass tonight at work. I ain't think she would try to get you killed."

"That's funny?"

"You still alive, ain't you? You always got next time."

"Nah, I don't. That shit fucked me up. So much that I needed to go see Mama," I said and watched his body stiffen. "Yeah, bitch-ass nigga. I had to walk in and see what the fuck you did to my mama, nigga."

"I ain't do shit," he denied coldly.

"I saw it on the cameras. You know you're the reason she installed them in the first place? And changed her locks? She didn't think you'd actually hurt her. She was more fearful that something you did would come back to haunt her. But you were her demon. I saw you beat her to death. You ain't got nothing to say about it?" I asked, feeling the lava-hot tears roll down my cheeks.

"Yeah, I do, actually. *Fuck* that bitch. Fuck her. I got tired of hearing her damn mouth. Now, I don't have to. And I know you did like a good boy, like you always do, and deleted the footage. So, I'm good."

"Nah, I deleted the footage so I could send you to hell myself," I said, and my fist connected with his jaw before he saw it coming.

His head flew to the side, but he stabilized himself quickly and threw a haymaker back at me. Thankfully, I could dodge it and send one flying back at him. I connected with his face again, causing him to stumble to the left. Theo had always been the strongest sibling, but I was the fastest. I hadn't gotten into a fist fight with him since we were kids, and he always won. But right then and there, I felt like I had super Saiyan energy. We went blow for blow, with me landing more than him.

When he tried to go for his gun, I hit him with a gut punch and snatched it from his waist, throwing it far out of his reach. I continued to plunder into him the same way he'd done our mother, until he fell to the ground. His eye had already swollen up, and he had a deep gash above his eyebrow from one of the rings I wore. When he was on the ground, I didn't stop there. I began stomping him out until he stopped trying to get up. Finally, he had no choice but to lie there because he had no energy left. I only stopped to catch my breath, and when I did, he laughed. Even while he was in pain, he laughed.

"So . . . This is what she felt like when I killed her," he said and laughed again.

"What the fuck is wrong with you?"

"Nothing is wrong with me. I'm perfect," he said.

"Tell the devil that," I said, pulling out my gun and aiming it at his face to end him forever.

The sound of a gun cocking filled the room, and I froze because it wasn't mine. I turned around and saw a man I'd never seen before aiming a gun at my head. Although I didn't know him, there was something familiar about his eyes.

"That's *my* kill, so I'ma have to ask you to back away," he said.

"Nah, this nigga killed our mama. This is *my* kill."

"You're his brother?" he asked.

"Yeah."

"Well, this motherfucka killed my dad. I want his soul."

I looked back down at Theo, who was squinting to get a good look at the man. He gave a bloody smile and began laughing hysterically while clutching his chest in pain.

"Lawyer Allun Halloway? The square? You a gangster now?" he asked the stranger.

"Nah, not now. *Been.* And I don't go by Allun. I go by Dawg," he said. When I looked at Theo, he had a shocked look on his face.

"Dawg? *You're* Dawg? The ghost?"

"A real gangster knows how to hide in plain sight. I'm only showing my face for real now because you have a debt to pay in blood. And you took something else from me. Where's my sister? Where's Amber? I heard her get jumped. That's why I'm here."

It was my turn to be shocked. It was then that I realized where I recognized his eyes from. They were Amber's. I remembered Theo saying something about wanting to punish Amber, and my blood ran cold again. I turned my gun back to Theo.

"You did something to my shorty too?" I shouted. "Where is she?"

"I ain't do shit to that bitch, and I ain't kill your daddy. I killed my mama, though."

"Liar. I saw you on camera. I saw you run out of the firm with your gun out the same time my pops was killed."

"He . . . He was dead when I got there," Theo said. "I had my gun out in case whoever did it was still in there. I was there to kill him, though, but somebody got to it before me."

"Who?"

"I don't know. But a silver or gray G-Wagon was pulling out when I was pulling in."

There was only one person I knew who had a silver G-Wagon. I looked back at Dawg as the realization came over his face.

"Jimmy," we both said in unison.

"That nigga got my sister," Dawg said, and I could hear the slight panic in his voice.

"Why would he take Amber?" I asked, and he furrowed his brow at me.

"How you even know my sister, nigga?"

"I just said it. That's my shorty. And if that nigga Jimmy has her, he's heartless. He killed my brother."

"I know."

"You was behind that too?" I asked, switching aim on my gun to Dawg, who still had his pointed at me.

"No. I ain't have no parts in that. But even if I did, y'all threw the first bullet with it. He retaliated. I know why he would take Amber, but I just don't know why he would kill my dad."

"Why would he take her?"

"Because I'm starting my own operation. He's trying to hurt me for bossing up. He'll kill her. I gotta get to her." He forgot all about wanting to kill Theo and turned on his heels to rush out the door.

"I'm coming too," I said, following him.

"I hope she's dead when y'all get there," Theo said weakly.

"And I hope you burn for eternity," I said, turning back to him with my raised gun.

I squeezed the trigger three times and made sure my bullets entered his head. There would be no more Theo Lavy.

Chapter Twenty-seven

Darryl

The Past

When Theo left the office, I felt very uneasy. I didn't like being bullied or forced into doing things I didn't want to do. However, I took his threat very seriously. There was something about the boy's eyes that wasn't right. I didn't see it before, but I did now. He was dangerous. His sudden appearance had thrown me off so much that I almost forgot why I'd come into the office on the weekend. I rarely ever did that, especially if I could work from home. But I wanted a private setting to address the situation.

The sound of a ding took me out of my head and brought me back to reality. I heard footsteps approaching my office, and I clasped my hands together. I removed any troubled thoughts about Theo from my mind and focused on the person who had just stepped into my office. Jimmy Flaco, Dawg's best friend, smiled at me charmingly, like he'd done growing up. He respectfully held out his hand, and I stood up and firmly shook it. When Theo had come in, I thought he was Jimmy, since I'd called him and asked him to meet me at the firm.

"How you doing, Mr. Halloway?"

"I can't complain. Just beating these cases daily."

"I know that's right," he said with a grin.

"Take a seat, why don't you?" I said and motioned to the chair across from me.

"All right," Jimmy replied.

I took notice of his proper speech. The boy must have forgotten I'd watched him grow up. I knew he was as ghettofied as they came. I knew the streets were his home, but I never knew how deep in them he truly was until Jeffrey told me what he saw. I kept my composure, but it was then that I saw him for the fake that he was. I believed Jeffrey. He wouldn't lie to me. He saw who and what he saw. Still, I wanted to know some things.

"I'm sure you're wondering why I called you here this afternoon."

"It was a bit of a surprise. I thought something had happened to Dawg."

"Dawg is okay, but this does pertain to him . . . and you."

"What's going on?"

"It hit me recently that you've been in our lives for a long time," I started. "You've stayed the night at my house. My daughter considers you a second brother, and as much as I've fed you growing up, I consider you like a second son."

"Thank you, sir."

"Mm-hmm. I also know that as you became adults, Dawg's busy schedule could have made it hard for the two of you to keep your close bond, but you are still close to this day."

"True."

"My question is, how close?" I asked and gave him a stern look.

"What are you trying to ask, Mr. Halloway? Are you insinuating we're gay?"

"No, that's not what I'm saying at all. I guess I'll rephrase the question and be blunt so as not to waste your time or mine. I know you're in the streets, Jimmy. I'm not sure how far or if you deal drugs. But I know for a fact you're a killer." As I spoke, I saw his facial expression go from pleasant to cold.

"I don't know where you're getting your information from, Mr. Halloway."

"I'm a lawyer, Jimmy. And the one thing I notice is that you didn't deny the insinuation, which is one of the first silent admissions of guilt. Also, I have an eyewitness who saw you murder Cordell Lavy."

"Where's your proof of that?"

"As I told you, I have an eyewitness to what you did. And I'm sure there's a beat-up Impala somewhere full of your DNA and gun residue," I told him.

"Mmm. Okay." He nodded. "So, you called me here to blackmail me or something?"

"I called you here to ask how involved my son is with you," I asked calmly, and he began to laugh.

"How involved? How involved, you say? That nigga is in just as deep as me." I listened as the proper etiquette left once I knew who he was. "We've been moving weight together since we were in high school. He only moved out because he couldn't hide it good anymore. He only became a lawyer to wash his money."

"Interesting," I said, keeping my composure, although it hurt like hell to realize that I didn't know that side of my son. Many of his words and stances on things were beginning to make sense to me.

"Your beloved, perfect son? He's a drug dealer and . . . he's a killer, just like me. The only difference is he decided to live in the shadows. I'm bold enough to be outside for real," Jimmy told me. "You don't even know who the fuck was living under your roof. But you're here judging me for handling my business."

"I might not have known that part about my son's life, but I know he's nothing like you. You're cold-blooded, and you disgust me."

"He should too then."

"No, surprisingly, he doesn't. Because after all this time, my son has been able to balance two lives while you barely have a grip on one," I told him with humor in my eyes. "I'm realizing as you speak that, yes, I look down on what ruined my life as a child. But when it comes to my son? I've just always wanted him to be the best at what he's good at. And I realize now that I can't control his life because he will do what he wants anyway. Also, if he ever made the mistake of doing something as foolish as you did, at least he has a good lawyer in his corner. Get the fuck outta my office. And stay away from my family. Also, remember, I know something you don't want anyone else to know."

I waved him away. I could tell he didn't like my flex of dominance or my dismissal of him. Regardless, he got up and walked out. When he was gone, I took a deep breath. I'd gotten all the answers I needed. I understood why Dawg was late to work so many times, and I understood why he didn't want to represent Theo. My son was . . . a drug dealer. And Theo was his competition. They said that sometimes your kids were attracted to the life you hated, especially when you forced your own desires on them. Maybe I had some accountability in both of my children's life decisions. I couldn't blame myself because they both had turned out pretty damned good, and when it came to Dawg, surprisingly, the shock was the only feeling I had. The disappointment hadn't hit me yet. Nor did I think it would. Being mad at him would only push him away from me. Being a father was about finding solutions. I couldn't completely support him, but I could protect him in any way I knew how.

I turned to my desk computer and opened my files. Eventually, my son would know I knew about his secret life, and I would have to give him tough love about it. But when I was dead and gone, I wanted him to know I saw him, and I loved him anyway.

I opened the documents containing my will and quickly amended a few sentences. When I finished, I sat back and smiled. I was so busy looking at proof of my own personal growth that I hadn't heard the door chime again or the footsteps leading down to my office. By the time I did and looked up, Jimmy was already back inside my office with a gun pointed at my head.

"You know what, Mr. Halloway? You're right. You do know something that I don't want anyone else to know. And I don't trust you, so I guess you've gotta go."

The last thing I saw was the slight fire burst from his gun before everything went black.

Chapter Twenty-eight

Amber

"Please, don't," I begged, looking at the gun in Jimmy's hand.

I couldn't believe I'd been kidnapped by someone I considered family—a bonus brother. I always knew he was a hothead, but I never thought he would do anything to hurt me or Dawg. I was bound on the floor, and I'd scooted to the corner of the room I was being held in . . . partly because Jimmy was pointing a gun in my direction, and the other part was because there was already a dead body occupying the room. Tied to a chair was a headless, naked body. He was missing all of his limbs and even his penis. Jimmy was sick, and I knew he was going to kill me, but I just wanted to know why.

"Why are you doing this?"

"You're his heart, and I want it broken," he said simply with a shrug.

His voice was cold and steady. I knew that meant he was standing firm in his decision, and there was nothing I could do. I sat there staring into the familiar face of a man that I loved deeply, and he stared back at me with hatred.

"But . . . I love you. My family loves you."

"You don't love shit. Your daddy told me exactly how he felt about me right before I killed him."

I almost choked on my next breath. *Jimmy* had killed Daddy? But why would he do something so terrible? Daddy had cared for him like a bonus son growing up. He'd vacationed with us, stayed countless nights with us, and built bonds with us. I couldn't understand it. Little did I know, he was about to tell me.

"Dawg just had the perfect life. He didn't struggle. He didn't need to be in the streets. He got in them because of me. This shit was play to him, but it was real to me. I ain't grow up having shit y'all had. And when my brother died, everything was supposed to be mine. Dawg was in the shadows for a reason. He knew his place then, but not anymore."

"What do you mean?" I asked, trying to keep him talking.

Behind my back, I was working my wrists out of the binds he had on me without him knowing. He was so hysterical and focused on telling his story that he didn't even notice my shoulders slightly moving up and down.

"He's trying to be the plug when that's supposed to be me. He ain't finna be my connect when *I'm* the one who brought him into this shit."

"Dawg is the reason you even have an operation. When Jake died, you couldn't even cop from the connect. He's the only one who could because of how you're acting like right now. Crazy."

"Shut the fuck up," he shouted, and I flinched when he jabbed the gun in my direction. "You don't know shit about me for real. You don't know how losing your first best friend feels. The only one to ever have your back. I thought that person was Dawg, but he's a snake just like this dead motherfucka."

He motioned toward the dead body. I assumed the person had done something to get on Jimmy's bad side.

Clearly, he had because, if he didn't, I was sure he would still be alive. I took a deep breath and tried to hide the pain of the rope burning the skin on my wrists.

"My brother isn't a snake. He's just . . . better than you," I said, knowing that probably wasn't helping my case, but I couldn't sit there and let him down-talk Dawg like he was something he wasn't.

"Then why wouldn't he cut me in? Why he wanna be over me?"

"Because you can't take everybody to the top, Jimmy," I said, shaking my head. "And if you killed my daddy? I pray Dawg never finds out because he's gonna do you worse than you did this person right here."

"He can bring it then. Your daddy had to go. He threatened me with some very private business, and we all know lawyers are damn near police with the right ammunition. Sorry, but not sorry. I still don't know how he found that shit out, but it doesn't matter now, does it?"

I couldn't blink the tears away as I thought about Jimmy being the one to shoot and kill Daddy. I jumped when I heard the gun cock back and felt warm tears streaming down my face. He didn't care about what I had to say. I was hoping that it wouldn't have to come to that. I was hoping that my gift of gab would save me. I wished I could just go back and change it all. But it was too late. Fate had already played its hand for me, and it was time to sweep the cards off the table.

As I stared into his eyes, our time together as kids flashed before mine. My brother and my friend. It was time to say goodbye, and I closed my eyes right as so many shots rang out. I also heard my high-pitched scream, knowing I was dead.

But then I realized that if I were dead, I wouldn't be able to scream. I opened my eyes and looked down at my body. I didn't have a single gunshot wound. My lip was trembling as I looked up and saw Jimmy's body staggering forward. A wide-eyed look was frozen on his face, and his mouth was slightly opened. The gun he had in his hand had fallen to his side, and the front of his jersey turned red. He gave one last slight sound out of his mouth before falling facedown right before me.

I gasped, not wanting the gun to go off in his hand, but it didn't. I looked tearfully at the entrance of the door and saw both Dawg and Myleek standing there, holding smoking guns.

"Tink," Dawg said, and he ran to me first.

He lifted me, wrapped his arms around me, and held me tightly. I buried my head in his neck and allowed myself to sob freely. He rocked me for a few moments before pulling back.

"How did you know where to find me?" I asked and then looked from Dawg to Leek. "And how are you two here together?"

"It's a long story," Leek said as Dawg untied my arms and ankles. When completely free, I threw my arms around Leek, and he kissed me. "I was scared as fuck, shorty."

"I was too," I said, and he held me. I looked at Dawg. "Theo didn't kill Daddy."

"I know," he said and glared down at Jimmy's dead body. "*He* did. Now we're left to pick up the pieces."

"We will," I said and grabbed both of their hands. "Now, let's get out of here. I can't look at these bodies for much longer, and that one over there is starting to stink."

We left the trap, and on the way to Razberry, they filled me in on what had happened after Jimmy snatched me from the club. I listened to the pain in Myleek's voice as he described the gory details of his mother's murder at the hands of Theo. Her own son killed her, and Leek had to kill his brother, which was why we were on the way back to the club to take care of the body.

I was sad for Leek. He was like me now, but a little worse off. He wasn't just an orphan now. He was the last of his immediate family. My heart was heavy for all of us. We'd all been through so much recently, and the only things that would heal our hearts were time and each other. That is, if Leek chose to stick around.

After a while, nobody had anything to say, and we rode quietly. They were in the front seats, and I was spread out in the back. I was exhausted and, at the same time, filled with so many emotions that all I wanted to do was rest.

"Look," Dawg finally said, breaking the silence. I lifted my head, but to my surprise, he was looking over at Leek. "I don't know if this shit means we're bonded by blood, and this probably ain't the right time, but—"

"Business must continue."

"Exactly. Nobody cares about our pain. They only care about our work, and with Theo dead—"

"And Jimmy gone—"

"It's us. I'm taking over my Cuban connect's operation in Florida, but I'd still like to have my hand in Atlanta. And I don't know what you two have going on for real, but I don't think Amber is trying to leave you."

"Ain't," I added, and they laughed.

"I'll fuck with you," Leek said to him. "But there's a lot I gotta clean up first, starting with my brother's body back at Razberry. I always had my brothers to help me with this shit. Now, it's just me."

"After what you did for me tonight, and if you play your cards right with my sister, you might have just gained a brother for life."

I let them continue talking as my head fell back on my arms. My life wasn't a fairy tale. It was unconventional and dysfunctional. It was full of secrets and bloodshed, which would probably continue. But it was my life. Sometimes, when a person chooses to follow their heart, it leads to turmoil. But there was always a light at the end of the path if you believed there would be. Recently, I learned to become one with loss and sadness to appreciate the hope for happiness again. I was still learning. I didn't know where my path would take me after everything that had happened, but in a world of drugs, guns, tricks, and hoes, the end of the tunnel had to have a pot of gold.

The End